Cupid In Bondage

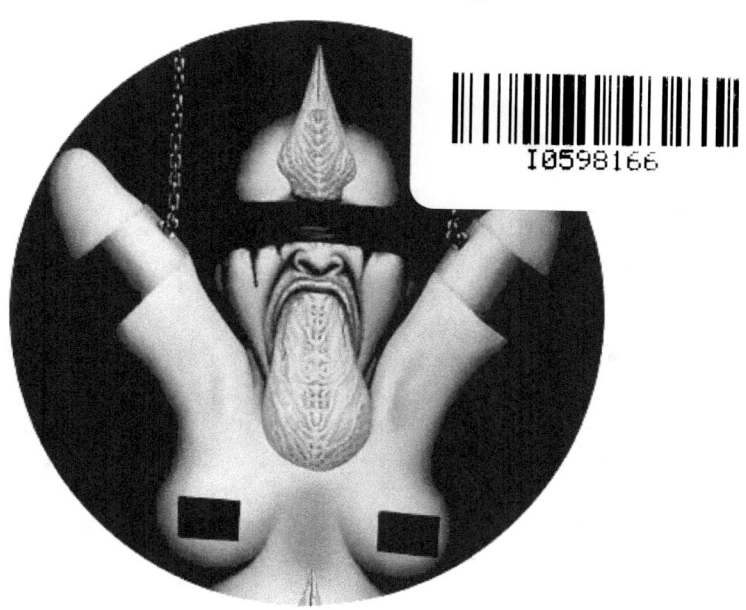

Wrath James White

deadite
press

deadite press

DEADITE PRESS
P.O. BOX 10065
PORTLAND, OR 97296
www.DEADITEPRESS.com

AN ERASERHEAD PRESS COMPANY
www.ERASERHEADPRESS.com

ISBN: 1-62105-169-2

Printed in the USA.

To Mom

**DEADITE PRESS BOOKS
BY WRATH JAMES WHITE**

The Book of a Thousand Sins
Population Zero
His Pain
Hero (with J.F. Gonzalez)
Like Porno for Psychos
Son of a Bitch (with Andre Duza)
Poisoning Eros (with Monica J. O'Rourke)

CONTENTS

COMING OUT KINKY

ON EXTREME HORROR, BDSM, PRIMAL SEX, AND WHY SHE CALLS ME DADDY AND I CALL HER BABY

As a writer of visceral and extreme fiction, one of my biggest challenges is separating myself, in the eyes of my readers, from the reprehensible characters in my novels and short stories. Surely the author of such gore-soaked depravities as *Succulent Prey, The Resurrectionist, Population Zero,* and *His Pain* must have some deep-seated emotional issues, right? You cannot write about cannibalism, rape, torture, and dismemberment so graphically and convincingly without harboring some secret desire to perform these acts or (gulp!) having actually performed them, right? Well, wrong.

All the horror authors I know—even extreme horror authors—are well-adjusted members of society and some of the nicest people you would ever want to meet. That includes guys like Edward Lee, Brian Keene, Jesus Gonzalez, Bryan Smith, Jack Ketchum—and me. We are not slavering, psychopathic fiends. I do not actually perform any of the violent and loathsome acts depicted in my horror fiction, nor do I fantasize about doing them. They are not reflective of some deep desire to sadistically rape, torture (unless it's consensual), or kill. After I write a brutal murder scene, it is not uncommon for me to sit and watch cartoons with my daughters. My oldest daughter was actually an infant, asleep on my lap or cradled in my arms, through most of the writing of *His Pain* including *that* scene (yeah, that one.) That said, I'm afraid this collection may just blur that distinction even further.

Some of the erotica tales in this collection are, in fact, true. Not the erotic horror (those works are clearly fiction), but some of the BDSM stuff is real. It will probably surprise no one who has read my work to discover that I'm a kinky son of a bitch. The depth and breadth of my kinks and fetishes I prefer to keep personal, though you will discover a few of them within these pages. And just as horror authors are often wrongly characterized as demented ghouls, so too do the sexually deviant have to contend with the common perception that deviance is malevolence or, at the very least, madness. A misconception that is equally erroneous and ill-informed.

One thing that some may find confusing, shocking, or even worrisome is the Daddy Dom/babygirl dynamic frequently alluded to in my writing. Even some within the BDSM community are confused by it, because it has so many variations and, of course, the terms "Daddy" and "Baby" when used sexually, are encumbered by the disturbing connotations of incest and statutory rape. None of those connotations apply in the Daddy Dom/babygirl dynamic, to put your mind at ease. In fact, in my relationship dynamic, there is not even age play. I have no desire to be with a woman who pretends to be a little girl. That is not my particular kink. My kink is playing "Daddy" to a grown woman. But there are Daddy Doms who play with "Littles" (women who affect the mannerisms and dress of little girls,) but that is not to imply that they have any interest in actually having sex with a child. They are not pedophiles. Their kink is being with a grown woman who acts like a child. A very important distinction. That is what they find sexy. The babygirls I know range in age from their early twenties to their late forties and early fifties.

A pedophile would have no interest in these women, even if they were wearing diapers and using baby-talk. Their bodies are still mature, adult bodies, and no amount of role-play can change that. So, when you see "Daddy" and "Baby" being used throughout some of my erotica, it is not in reference to anything incestuous or pedophilic. These are merely terms of endearment between consenting adults.

Oh, and I guess I should explain what a "Primal" is, for those who don't know, since, in addition to identifying as a Daddy Dom, I also identify as a Primal, and there are frequent references to "Primal sex" throughout my writing. As I explained on a kink website I belong to:

"I am a Primal as well as a Daddy. I bite. I growl. I roar. For me, "primal" does not mean that I am channeling my spirit animal or anything so metaphysical. It means that I want to tear you apart with my bare hands and teeth. Primal defines the emotions behind, as well as the physicality of, my style of play. I do not identify as a wolf or a lion or any other animal. The monster inside me is unique to the animal kingdom. My baby girl soothes the beast in me, but she also brings it out. She likes the monster. She is the beauty to my beast. "

Here's an excerpt from a blog post I wrote that I think explains it fairly well:

"Being a primal means being in touch with the most savage side of our nature. It means playing with the dormant animal instinct(s) to hunt, fight, and even rape and kill, but if you can control it well enough to hold a job, then you can control it during play...Primal play is not as calm and restrained as other types of BDSM play. It often looks more like some sort of physical assault than the more refined and organized sadism of most scenes. Whips and floggers are often eschewed in favor of teeth and nails. Wrestling a lover into submission and pinning him or her down takes the place of ropes and chains. When there's blood, it isn't [usually] from a sterilized needle or scalpel, but from a bite or a scratch..."

Most sadomasochists I know, whether they identify as primals or not, prefer primal sex to vanilla sex. The growling, biting, scratching, and wrestling is just...well...fucking hot! In fact, I have known few women, kinky or vanilla, who didn't consider it some of the best sex they've ever had. To coin a popular phrase in the kink community: "Bite marks and bruises are just love notes written in flesh." That goes for welts and cuts as well.

Was combining erotic horror and BDSM erotica a wise move considering all the misconceptions sadomasochism already has to combat, not to mention those of horror authors? Who knows? The future will be my judge, but taking risks is what I do. My willingness to push conventional boundaries and defy taboos is no doubt what made you pick up this book in the first place. But, by placing the two side by side, I'm hoping to show the distinct difference between them, the stark contrast between sadism and masochism that is safe, sane, loving, and consensual, and true psychopathy. If I have done my job, by the time you reach the end of this little collection, the differences should be obvious. It should be evident that not every sadist is a psychopath or a sociopath. This particular sadist is, in fact, quite compassionate and romantic. Some, including my babygirl, would say exceptionally so.

My babygirl, who I am proud to say is also my fiance', is my very life and breath. I adore her like no woman I have ever known and would never do anything to hurt her (without her consent, of course.) In fact, most people in the BDSM lifestyle are extraordinarily loving and affectionate, even while paddling, flogging, whipping, caning, cutting, spanking, electrocuting, and setting one another on fire. Some of the most open, honest, respectful, reciprocal, passionate, romantic, and communicative couples I know tie each other up with ropes and chains and spank and flog one another regularly.

If you weren't already prepared and, I would dare say, eagerly anticipating the extreme, horrific, visceral scenes of sexual violence portrayed in my erotic horror stories, you probably would not have purchased this particular book. I have other books that are far less sexual. Far more cerebral and philosophical, though perhaps no less violent. But you chose this one. So, as you read this twisted collection of terror and perversity, savagery and debauchery, understand that you are getting a simultaneous look into my imagination and my life. I do hope you are able to distinguish between the two.

—Wrath James White

somewhere near Austin, Texas
September, 20, 2014.

HARDER, DADDY

She is so small. At 37-years-old, she is only slightly bigger than an adolescent in stature. Though, she would argue that point.

"I'm not that small!"

But I have seen her wearing my daughter's clothes...my youngest daughter's.

Her skin is so soft. It is easy to imagine biting into it, easy to imagine that it would have the consistency of marshmallow or oven-fresh bread, and be filled with something sweet, like butter cream frosting or apples and cinnamon. I am almost afraid she will break, shatter and melt away like an ice cream sculpture. So, I slide inside her slowly, taking my time. I swallow my growls, keep the beast in its cage. I try to control the lecherous, sadistic lust, enticing me to split her wide and pound against her cervix. But she feels So. Good.

Unable to hold myself back, I thrust a little harder and wait for her to squeal in that delicious harmony of pleasure and discomfort I have come to expect from women.

Instead, she whispers breathlessly:

"Harder, Daddy."

Are you sure? Do you know what you are asking? I'm not just your average punk off the street. I'm a goddamn monster in the bedroom! I'm a destroyer! I'm a fuckin' beast! Are you sure? Are you ready for this?

"Harder, Daddy!" She says insistently.

I raise up to a push-up position, balancing myself on my knuckles and the tips of my toes and crash down on her like a tsunami colliding against the beach. Again and again, harder, faster.

You like that? Is this what you wanted? You like that?

"Oh, Yes! Harder, Daddy!"

You have got to be kidding me? I'm too old for this. I'm not in my twenties anymore. I have to go to work in the morning. My back hurts. I don't know how much longer I can hold myself up. What am I talking about? I'm Ivan the Terrible! Attila the Hun! Alexander the Great! I'm a conqueror and this pussy belongs to me!

The growl rumbles up from my chest and echoes through the dark room like a revving engine. I roll her onto her belly, bite down on the back of her neck and pound in deeper, harder, trying to drive through her, to burrow through her flesh into her soul.

"Harder, Daddy! Harder!"

I seize her by the pigtails, holding them both in one hand and smacking her ass with the other, not softly, playfully, but hard smacks that redden her flesh and leave livid bruises. I bite her shoulder, sinking my teeth in deep. I hear her gasp, feel that splash as her loins unleash a river. She loves the pain. She feeds on my savagery. I see the shine in her eyes as the dopamine begins to flow and lust sparkles in those brilliant blue and gray orbs like amphetamines.

"Harder, Daddy!"

I squeeze her throat until her breath becomes a hoarse whisper. My cock is harder than it's been in years. Like a club, a battering ram. She grunts with each thrust and claws the sheets.

I am a lion! A tiger! I'm a goddamn werewolf!

"Oh my God! You feel so huge! Harder, Daddy! Harder!"

Harder? Seriously?

I pull out. Slide down her back, kissing and nuzzling her supple skin. Then I clutch her lovely ass, squeeze it in my hands, and roar as I bend down and seize a sizeable chunk of that tender globe of flesh between my teeth and bite down so hard I can almost feel my teeth touch. I thrash my head back and forth, tugging at the succulent flesh like a shark in a feeding frenzy. She cries out, and her cries increase the monster's voluptuous appetite. I bite again and again, tearing at her as if trying to separate flesh from bone.

I am King Kong! I am Godzilla!

I raise up, admiring the lovely bites and bruises on my baby's ass. I smack it again and watch those lovely half-moons wobble, hear that quick intake of breath as I add to the profusion of bruises with a hand that nearly engulfs her entire ass. I spank her until I can no longer contain myself and have to feel that sweet pussy again. I spoon with her, with one hand around her throat and the other again clutching her pigtails, my teeth once more clamped onto the back of her neck as I vent my furious lust inside her, my cock hammering the gates of paradise like a horde of demons. Her moans reach their apex, and I can feel the moment of my arrival like a massive furnace boiling to critical pressure, preparing to release in a tremendous explosion.

I roll her onto her back and stare into her eyes. I can see her studying my face, trying to find her sweet, loving Daddy in the ravenous beast now plundering her sex. But I am gone. I am lost in my desires. Her face is contorted in salacious agony, and it is like a drug to me. I feed on her pain like a vampire.

"Open your mouth," I growl and she complies.

I pull out and bathe her tongue, her lips, her cheeks, chin, neck, and breasts in my seed. And she smiles, looking so satisfied, happy that she has pleased her daddy. I collapse beside her, breathing heavily, exhausted, spent. She is almost giddy.

"That was so amazing! Oh my god!"

I nod. It was good.

"But next time...can you do it harder?"

You have got to be fucking kidding me.

CUPID IN BONDAGE

Inside my hand
a leather strap
fifty times
across your back
just to see if you can writhe
as sexy as you dance
to see if your screams
are more honest
than your words

Between my teeth
a razor blade
shallow cuts
that heal and fade
just to see if you can learn
to love the pain
to see if you can
ever
trust again

Shackled to the bedpost
straining against your bonds
just to show you that the world

is not your friend
to prove to you
that love
is not a game.

THIS IS
MY BLOOD

I give communion
Spill thick upon her tongue
Slither down her throat

My lust
like bile
Scalding her esophagus
Burning deep within

I coat her lovely face
Her engorged breasts
Her perfect ass

I empty myself
Into her
Onto her

I become her faith
and boil in her belly
with the other parasites.

LARGER THAN GOD

He walked down the street drawing stares from the throngs of middle-class suburbanites who were not used to seeing a massive black man in leather walking through their neighborhood. He wore a quarter-length leather coat with no shirt and a silver chain with a dried cobra head fashioned into a charm hanging from it that draped down between his tremendous muscular pecs. His black jeans hung low off his hips like a gunslinger. They would have revealed the tops of his underwear had he been wearing any. Now they revealed where the treasure trail of hair that traveled down from between his pecs terminated in dark pubic hair. His black police-issue riding boots had been recently shined, and they glistened in the morning sun as he strode through the streets like he owned them. His head was freshly shaved and shined with sandalwood-scented oil. He looked like some combination of Shaft and the Candyman.

His complexion was nearly identical to his attire, shiny black. His skin was the very absence of light. Sunlight found its death there, absorbed into his ebon flesh like a black hole, a living shadow. His eyes blazed with a morality-negating appetite that seemed to charge the air around him with a violent sexuality. As large as his body was, it seemed ill equipped to contain the roiling passion boiling within him. It was as if someone had encased a hurricane in flesh.

He smiled as a fat, pale, soft-looking couple passed him, watching with cautious eyes. The woman stared a moment too long, purposely catching his eyes before dragging her gaze down his chest to his crotch area and back up to his eyes. Her lips parted breathlessly before she forced herself to turn away. He laughed. At six foot, five inches and roughly 235 pounds of carbonized steel, he knew what he must look like to the housewives and their soft and doughy husbands as they scrambled off to church with their kids. Everyone who saw him in this neighborhood either feared him, hated him, wanted to fuck him, or some combination of the three. He was used to it. He loved being the center of attention.

He was just passing the church when he spotted her. She was gorgeous in a way that seemed almost sinful while waiting to enter a church in this pristine neighborhood. He felt her from all the way across the street. He sensed her need; the hollowness in her that only he could fill. Nothing in that church could help her. But he could.

She had pale, milky-white skin, like vanilla ice cream or untouched snow. Her hair was long, black, and purposely wild, styled that way, like the heroin in some type of action film. Her lips were naturally pouty, giving her the look of a spoiled child. She had full hips, a large, round ass, and a small waist. Built like a woman. Not like those anemic fashion models, so skinny they're almost sexless—no hips, no ass, barely any breasts, more like very pretty boys than women. She was beautiful. Her eyes were gorgeous and intense. He walked across the street and joined the crowd. It seemed like a perfect day for church.

He sat down in the pew beside her. She kept glancing over at him and each time found him staring back at her, not turning away, not masking the hunger in his eyes, not pretending to be doing anything less than what he was...—

21

lusting. He noticed, with no small amount of delight, that the silver chain around her neck was in fact a dog collar; a choke chain. She was owned by someone. Some Dom who was probably not worthy of her. Now he was certain he wanted her and knew with even greater certainty that she needed him.

She caught him looking at her again, and this time he smiled and wet his lips with his tongue. She smiled back.

He leaned over and whispered in her ear.

"Now what the hell are you doing in church?"

"What do you mean?"

"You know exactly what I mean." He reached out and tugged on her choke collar for emphasis.

She turned red and smiled coyly.

"My sexual preferences and religious beliefs are mutually exclusive. This church thing is part of my rehab. I was becoming a bit of a drunk. Drinking was the only way I could keep from sniffing heroin. This church sponsors a twelve-step program that helped me get clean and sober. You know, they say you need a higher power in order to kick addiction. So since I was here already, I chose Jesus. He's as good a Higher Power as any."

"You used alcohol to help kick heroin and now you use Jesus to help kick alcohol? I'm jealous already."

"Jealous of what?"

"Of Jesus. I should've been here for you. I should've been your higher power." He leaned in close until his face was nearly touching hers, and it felt as if the smoldering heat of his gaze would singe her eyelashes. "It's not too late, is it?"

"What the hell do you mean? Too late for what?"

"Shhhhhhh! The pastor's speaking! I can't hear the sermon!" The blue-haired old ladies in front of them turned around and pinned them with angry stares.

"Churchgoers tend to be the most intolerant people," he whispered, loud enough for the old woman to hear.

"Come talk to me outside."

She looked around and then stood up, stepping over the other parishioners as she scrambled out of the pew. She walked with the tremendous hyper-muscular, leather-clad black man with the snake's head dangling against his naked chest, out the door and into the church's vestibule as angry and concerned stares followed them.

"You don't need a fantasy, a phantom—that's all this church can offer you." He grabbed her hand and ran it over his bare chest and down over his rippled abs. "You need a Master who is real flesh and blood, who can really be there for you, to answer your prayers. Not just some amorphous ideology with a supreme being that you never get to see or touch or feel. Who exists only in your lovely head."

"I have a Master. His name is Master Craig. He collared me last month."

"And what has he done for you since?"

"We play. I serve him. I'm a service slave."

"How ..exactly...do you serve him?"

"I come by in the morning before work and make him breakfast, iron his clothes, suck his cock, and then wash his dishes. After work, I come make him dinner, wash the dishes, and clean the kitchen, and then I vacuum the house and sometimes he fucks me. Sometimes he'll flog or cane me. It's good."

"Is it what you thought it would be? When you look at him, is he the object of worship you were expecting to find when you first entered this lifestyle? Am I? What has he taught you about yourself? About the world? How has he expanded your horizons? What has he done to earn your service?"

"He...he...I don't know."

He smirked and shook his head.

"And that's why you should be my slave. You don't need Jesus or this...Craig." He spat out the name like it tasted vile in his mouth. Then he smiled and pressed her palm to his chest again so she could feel his heart pound like some kind of heavy machinery at work within him. His obsidian eyes were soft and caring yet held a feral intensity, the way a lion looks at its cubs. "All you need is me."

"What are you, some kind of pimp?"

"Let me be your new divinity," he replied, ignoring her question.

She opened her mouth to speak and he kissed her...gently, no more than a light peck. But it was enough. Her mouth slammed shut and she just stood there staring into his dark savage eyes.

"You need me. So I am here for you. Would you refuse me?"

She shook her head slowly at first as she continued to stare, hypnotized, into his eyes. Then her eyes took on a more determined look, and she shook her head again with more certainty.

"No, Sir. No fucking way I can refuse you, Sir. You're beautiful! My god, you're beautiful! I've never seen anything—anyone—like you. You are what a Dom should look like. How he should talk."

"Beautiful is not all that I am. Let me show you."

"Yes," she replied breathlessly. She took his hand and led him downstairs to the church basement where they normally held the AA meetings. It was empty so they sat down to talk.

"What is your name anyway, Sir?"

"You don't need to call me sir."

"Master?" She asked uncertainly.

"Lord."

"Yes, Lord. My name is Glenda."

"So tell me Glenda. Who are you?"

They talked for nearly an hour with Lord asking most of the questions and her providing most of the answers. He

24

preferred to let his past remain a mystery for the time being. They exchanged phone numbers and continued talking for another hour. They knew that pretty soon the congregation would be letting out and they were bound to be interrupted.

Lord pulled her close and kissed her eagerly, sucking her bottom lip and her tongue, running his huge hands across her thighs, ass, and up her back. He wanted to make love to her right there in the church and he could feel her desire as well. He started to remove her shirt and she pulled away from him.

"You don't want me?" he inquired with a look that seemed more curious than hurt or disappointed.

"We can't do it in the church, my Lord?"

His eyes narrowed, eyebrows furrowed. He grabbed her by the throat in one massive hand and squeezed just hard enough to make breathing difficult, but not impossible.

"We can do it wherever I say we can. How else will I know that you don't still love him more than me? Am I your Lord? Or is he?" He asked pointing at the crucifix on the wall.

Glenda wanted to protest. She wanted to tell this man that she hardly even knew him so how could she love him? But there was something in her heart, in her very soul, that stirred under his gaze and swooned at the sound of his voice, something that leaped and soared when his skin touched hers. She had known love before and it had paled in comparison to this.

Still, she remained cautious. She pulled away from him.

"I know what you're going to do, Lord." She said. "You're going to get me all worked up and then just leave." Her bottom lip trembled as she spoke and her eyes swept the floor.

Lord smiled mischievously. He grabbed her by the hair and pulled her close, kissing her again, flexing his biceps as he held her against his hard muscular chest so she could feel the power in his arms, so she'd know that there was no escaping him, no denying him. He bit her bottom lip and then pulled her even closer, crushing the breath from her lungs for a second before relaxing and bending down to sink his teeth into her neck and kiss his way down between her milk-white breasts. She was helpless in his embrace. He reached under her shirt and ripped off her bra. Then he pulled her silk blouse over her head and began to suck her hard dark nipples circling them with his tongue and lightly nibbling them.

Upstairs the choir started up, singing some song about giving your heart to the Lord. It echoed through the floor as if the whole choir was in the room with them. The voices wailed and nearly shrieked out the chaotic gospel tune and it seemed to stir Lord's appetite even more. His kisses grew more urgent and insistent.

Glenda cooed softly as he unzipped her jeans and slid them down her smooth thighs kissing her soft belly as he knelt to slide them down to her ankles. He dragged his tongue up her thighs, between her thighs, up over her stomach, between her breasts, up her neck and into her mouth where she sucked it eagerly. As they kissed he slid his fingers up inside her, sliding his middle and index fingers into her silky, tight, wetness. His head was filled with the impassioned voices of the choir and he began to play her body like a musical instrument, working her clitoris with his thumb, listening for her breath to quicken, her moans to deepen, her legs to quiver.

She reached out to touch his erection and as much as he wanted her, needed her, he grabbed her wrist and jerked her arm behind her back growling out a single word.

"No. I asked you a question. Am I your Lord? Or is He?"

"You are my Lord."

He grabbed her other wrist and pulled that around in back of her as well pinning both wrists crushed together in one huge hand as he continued to make music from her flesh. He slipped his fingers out of her and slid them across her lips and then into her mouth where she sucked them clean, then he kissed her deeply savoring the taste of her sex on her tongue. He stepped back and admired her, standing there completely naked with her jeans down around her ankles. She looked so beautiful, so tender and innocent, so vulnerable.

She started to reach down and pull her jeans up.

"Don't move," he growled.

She stood up and hugged her arms over her chest subconsciously.

"Uh uh," He said shaking his head and she dropped her arms.

Her nipples were still hard and pointing right at him. Lord reached out and traced her left nipple with his finger making her shiver then he softly pinched it causing her to gasp.

"Beautiful," he said staring deeply into her eyes. "Very beautiful."

He stood there, staring at her for nearly a full minute. She shuffled nervously from one foot to the other with her hands clasped in front of her. She would look up into his eyes, smile nervously, and then drop her eyes when he didn't return her smile. She would start to cover her breasts with her arms and then remember and drop her arms back to her sides.

He reached into his jacket and uncoiled a long, black, single-tail whip. It was four feet long, 16 plaits, with a big triangular piece of leather where the fall and the cracker would normally be, like some hybrid between a signal whip and a dragon's tail.

"What's the safe words?" she asked automatically.

"Yellow and red, of course. Do you want it?"

"Please, my Lord."

He flicked it once. The tip barely grazed her nipple, but the whip made a loud "Crack!" Lord saw her entire body shiver. He cracked it again, once more just grazing her other nipple. Then he stepped closer. Half a step. This time when he cracked it, it bisected her nipple and drew blood. He waited to hear if she would use her safe word. She moaned and closed her eyes, her body still shivering. Her sex glistening with arousal.

"Turn around," he commanded.

She did as he commanded and he stepped closer and smacked her lightly on her sumptuous ass. He alternated between rubbing it and smacking it, each time smacking it harder than the last, He did the same to her upper back. When she was good and red, her flesh warm to the touch, he stepped back and once more let the whip fly. It sang threw the air and cracked against her skin, leaving a long welt on her left buttock, but not drawing blood.

Glenda hissed between clenched teeth, squeezing her eyes shut. Her body trembled. The next crack was millimeters away from her skin. It was as loud as a gunshot, and Glenda flinched. Lord smiled then cracked the whip again, striping her other ass cheek.

He striped her back and buttocks, drawing blood, reducing Glenda to tears, but she never used her safe word. She crumpled to the ground, breathing heavily and trembling.

Lord walked over to her and stood above her. He removed his cock and began to urinate on her."Who's your Lord?" he asked as he pissed in her hair.

"You are, my Lord."

"Look at me!" He barked.

She did as he commanded, catching a stream of his urine, full in the face as he continued to piss on her.

"Who. Is. Your. Lord?"

"You are, my Lord. You're my Lord. You're my only Master. I worship you!"

She bowed before him, kissing the tips of his boot.

Lord shook out a few last drops of urine onto the back of her head as she continued to kiss his boots. Then he tucked his cock back in his pants, reached out for the door, and unlocked it.

"I'll call you." He said and then he slipped out the door slamming it behind, leaving her kneeling on the floor, naked, aroused, bloodied, and covered in urine, alone in the church basement with the choir voices ululating insanely above her head.

***

Something about the music was not quite right, not quite holy, she thought. But she could not put her finger on it. As she heard his footsteps recede up the stairs and out of the church the choir began to die down. When they began their new song "Wade in the water" it was as if an entirely different choir were singing. None of the fanatical rapture that had been there previously remained. They sounded passionless and dreary in comparison.

Glenda was shaking with sexual tension as she quickly dressed and left the room. She took a deep breath, inhaling the crisp night air and steadying herself, quieting the riot of sensations radiating up from her loins as she walked up the church steps and out the front doors. The strong, ammonia scent of Lord's urine was all over her. She hadn't bothered trying to wash it off before stepping out into the night. She liked this reminder of her experience. The entire thing had been so bizarre. There had been no negotiation. No discussion of her limits, her desires, or her fetishes. He had simply done what he wanted to her and she had let him. Seeing him with that whip had taken all her words away. She had wanted, in that moment, to be owned by him, conquered by him. With Master Craig, she was a bit of a brat, burning his eggs on purpose, making his coffee too sweet, his pants too wrinkled, taking too long to shine his shoes, whining when he spanked her and trying to get away. Not this time. Not with Lord. His regal presence had commanded her obedience. No matter how much the whip had hurt, safe words were the furthest thing from her mind. She'd hit subspace faster than she could ever recall and was so high on endorphins she thought she was about to have an orgasm just from the whip cutting into her skin. She was so close when her stamina finally gave out and she'd fallen to the floor, no longer able to take the pain. Then, when she'd felt the warm, humiliating stream of his urine, splashing down upon her, looked up to see his huge, magnificent cock dangling above her head, raining piss, when he'd ordered her to declare him her Lord, to turn around so he could piss right in her face, she had never felt more submissive, never felt so thoroughly owned. Her only thoughts had been, *Fuck Master Craig. This is a real Master!*

She had no idea how long they had played, but it had been daylight when they entered the church, and now the sun was setting. The service was over and the parishioners were streaming out along with her. She could feel their hot accusatory gazes on her as she wound her way through the crowd. Some of them wrinkled their nose and waved their hands in front of their face as she passed by. She didn't give a fuck about any of them. She couldn't believe that she had once wanted to be one of them. They had no idea what real worship was.

That night she lay in bed dreaming about her new Lord, remembering the smell, the feel, the taste of him, that incredible body hard like an ebon statue, his skin a flawless curtain of night.

He didn't call her for two days. Each day was an agony for her.

On the third day he called her from the church.

"Hello?"

"Hello Glenda."

"Lord?"

"Do you have one of those little plaid skirts like the catholic school girls wear?"

"Yeah...um...yes, Lord I...I think so. Why?"

Lord could hear the nervousness, the excitement in her voice. He was excited too.

"Put it on and come down to the church."

"I just got home, Lord. " She protested half- halfheartedly.

"And don't wear any underwear." He hung up.

* * *

Lord told himself that he wasn't sure she'd come but he knew she would. What he didn't know was whether she'd follow his instructions and how he'd discipline her if she didn't.

She showed up half an hour later. She had on a white baby t-shirt with a hello kitty on the front, high heeled platform shoes...and a plaid catholic school skirt. Try as he might he couldn't suppress the smile.

It was already dark and the church was nearly empty except for the choir rehearsing upstairs. Lord took Glenda by the hand and led her through the church to the door that led back down to the basement. They descended the stairs in silence and Lord could feel her nervousness and apprehension.

When they entered the small darkened room he turned to look at her. She was fully though provocatively dressed this time but she still averted her eyes and shuffled nervously from foot to foot as if she were exposed.

"Come here." he wrapped one arm around her waist and pulled her close to him.

"So what is it with you and churches, Lord?"

He kissed her hungrily. Their hands danced over each other's bodies with wanton abandon. Lord cupped her small perfectly round breasts in his hands and traced her hardening nipples with his finger then he cupped her large but equally round ass in his other hand, sliding it underneath her skirt. She had followed instructions. Her ass was bare and smooth.

He let his hands slide down her thighs, delighting in the smooth supple feel of her naked skin. Then he slid his hands around to the front, up between her thighs, and felt the sweet moistness of her, sliding one finger and then another up inside her as she gasped with pleasure.

She tried to reach both hands down his pants, was thwarted by his belt and paused to unbuckle it, ripping it from the belt loops and tossing it across the room in her eagerness. She popped the button on his jeans as she ripped them open.

Lord almost wished that he had been wearing underwear. It would've been interesting to see what she would've done to them.

They covered each other in kisses as their hands flew across one another's bodies stroking, caressing, and removing clothing. Overhead, the choir kicked up again. It was the same song as the other day, the one about giving your heart to God, and it immediately rose to a deafening crescendo before crashing back down to earth. There was something almost erotic about it, orgasmic, with its many crescendos and wild shrieks and moans.

Glenda had heard some pretty impassioned singing from gospel choirs before but what she heard above her was like an acoustic orgy. She had never heard anything like this in a church before. She had never heard anything like it anywhere before. She tried to catch the lyrics and thought she heard references to biting and licking a woman's breasts but she knew that couldn't be right. She must have been confusing it with what she was doing or rather what was being done to her.

Whatever they were singing it seemed to be having an effect on Lord because once again his lovemaking became more aggressive. He sank his teeth into her neck and she scratched her fingernails over his massive pectoral muscles, clawing through his skin but curiously drawing no blood. She bent to lick and suck at his nipple. Causing him to purr and moan.

She began to kneel down to take him into her mouth but, in a moment of bizarre inspiration, he stopped her, lifted her off the ground 'til her legs were wrapped around his waist and their genitalia were crushed together. He spun her 180 degrees until her legs were now over his shoulder with her sweet silken folds inches from his face. Her head was right at his groin with his manhood brushing against her lips. She was surprised and confused as he had started to flip her around but when she realized where he was going with this maneuver she relaxed right into it. It was the first time she'd ever performed a sixty-nine standing up and she was eager and excited. For Lord, the maneuver was a perfect opportunity to once again demonstrate his strength, power, and control.

She had her legs bent, balanced on his shoulders, and he had both arms wrapped around her waist. The strength in Lord's arms was the only thing keeping her from hitting the concrete patio headfirst. She had to do more than merely trust him. She had to have faith; faith that he would cum and make her cum before his arms gave out.

He dove his tongue into her, lapping eagerly at her swollen clit sucking her labia and sliding his tongue in and out of her, fucking her with his tongue. Her hands stroked and caressed him while her tongue twirled all along his sex, bathing him in her saliva.

Her body shook. His tongue flicked across her clit faster and faster. His face was bathed in her juices. The pain in his shoulders and biceps seemed far off like it was happening to someone else and he was just feeling sympathy pain. He was in ecstasy, a near religious rapture, high on endorphins, adrenaline, the taste of Glenda, the feel of her. Nothing existed but her lips, her tongue, her dripping honey sweetness against his lips, and the orgasm he felt growing within, the convulsions her body was going through as her own orgasm jolted her like a thunder clap, pounded her like the surf against the shore.

Lord strained to hold her as she bucked and jerked in his arms, lost in her own pleasure, confident that she was safe in his arms, not the least bit concerned that he might drop her. She had faith. This ecstasy, this release, this abandonment of all control, all inhibition, all care was her new religion, and Lord was her high priest preparing to baptize her tongue with his seed.

Lord had to concentrate even more as his own climax struck him like a thousand volts. He could feel her tongue licking, her lips sucking, as his seed splashed into her mouth and she hungrily lapped up every drop of it.

When his own orgasm ended his knees wanted to buckle but he willed them to stand strong. His arms were on fire. His lower back was a tightening ball of agony. The muscles along his spine were bunching up into painful knots. It felt as if he were about to snap in half, but he held her firm. He wanted to relax his arms but continued to hold their painful contraction, pinning her in place as he pleasured her, and one orgasm after another shook her lovely body.

"Oh, Lord! Oh, Lord! Daddy! Yes! Yes! That feels so good, Daddy!"

When her orgasms finally subsided, Lord turned her back around to stand on her feet and, despite the fire in his biceps, resisted the urge to stretch them or shake them out or show any sign of his discomfort to her. He wanted to just let them hang at his sides, but he folded his arms across his chest, causing the painful contractions to increase and the muscles in his biceps to lock. Lord's face remained calm despite the pain. Curiously, the pain seemed to accentuate the pleasure he'd just experienced.

"Don't call me Daddy. If you must call me anything, call me Lord—and look at me when you say it. That way I know you mean me and not him," he said, nodding toward the crucifix on the wall with the tiny, gruesome effigy of Christ in his death throes affixed to it.

"Lord!" was all she said as she pulled her shirt back on and licked the remaining cum from her lips. She made sure to look at him when she said it. She walked over to retrieve his belt from where she had tossed it across the room.

Watching the slight ripple go through her perfectly round buttocks was arousing Lord again. He wanted more.

She brought him his belt, and his entire body shook with a barely controlled satyriacal fervor. A roiling furnace of passion burned within him. The animalistic fury of a hunger like no other man on earth possessed surged through his veins.

She smiled coyly and began to speak when something she saw in his eyes choked the words in her throat. She felt like a lamb peering into the eyes of a lion, burning alive in the voluptuous heat of his eyes. She took an involuntary step back.

Lord swept her up in his massive, sinuous arms and pinned her against the wall. He grabbed her by her shoulders and spun her around.

Pinning her head against the wall with his left hand while still wielding the leather belt in right, he rubbed the strap across her flesh. Her ass looked marvelous. Still holding her head pinned against the drywall, he lightly smacked the belt across her smooth pale skin, causing a quick intake of breath from Glenda. Her ass reddened almost immediately and jiggled deliciously. Lord smacked it again and slid his hand down between her thighs. She was even wetter now. He slid a finger up inside her and felt her contract around it. She moaned softly and began rocking back onto his hand.

The choir was in a frenzy. Their enraptured voices swirled about them like an aural maelstrom. Lord cracked the belt across Glenda's back harder, reddening the welts still healing from their last session and causing her to gasp in surprise. He cracked the belt across her ass even harder and then softly caressed her reddened skin.

"Oh, Lord, that hurts!" It wasn't a complaint.

Lord once again slid his hand between her legs, massaging her clit with his middle finger while lightly spanking her with the belt. She moaned and cried out loudly. Her cries of ecstasy joined the impassioned wailing of the choir and filled the halls. Lord was hard as tempered steel and lost in the whirlwind of sound and sensation as he brought the leather belt down onto Glenda's lovely ass again and again. Glenda let out another gasp of surprise as he slid himself up into her. He looped the belt through the buckle and slipped it over her head, wrapping it around her throat and cinching it tight like a noose. She started to choke and this only added to his excitement...—and hers. With one hand he held the belt like a leash and with the other he grabbed a handful of her hair. She was so wet, so tight; it was heaven inside her. Lord was drowning in the salacious sensation of flesh enveloped in wet, slippery flesh. The world tilted as the pleasure washed over him.

They stayed like that in the basement for what seemed like hours, fucking like crazed beasts in the grip of some instinctual rapture they were powerless to resist. When Glenda came, it was like her entire body went mad, jerking and twisting spasmodically. She wobbled like a newborn filly on shaky legs.

Lord was still painfully and urgently erect. Glenda gripped him in her hand and dropped to her knees. Her tongue teased tingles from his most sensitive nerves. The volcanic orgasm building within him erupted. Lord's body arched, and he let out a sound like a roar as the orgasm took hold of him and shook him like a G. I. Joe doll in the hands of a hyperactive child. He felt a pull at his heart and immediately beat it down. Her heart was for him. His would not, could not, be for her. He watched her kneel before him, eagerly taking his seed into her mouth as it splashed across her cheeks and dribbled off her chin like a sacrament. Lord felt like a god at the moment of communion. He looked at the crucifix on the wall again and stared right into Christ's eyes.

"This is my house! My house!" he yelled.

This is my body. This is my blood. She held out her tongue to catch the last drop of his semen as it dripped from his spent organ. Lord nearly swooned. It was absolutely beautiful. As always, he was overwhelmed by the purity of the act, the total giving over of oneself to the pleasure of another.

He reached down and lifted her to her feet.

"Now. Do you accept me as your Lord and savior?"

"I do."

"You will worship no one above me?"

"No one."

He reached into her chest, punched through her ribcage, and slowly pulled out her heart, feeling it rip free of the arteries and muscle tissue that held it.

"This is mine now."

"Yes, Lord." Her eyes were glazed with a profound love as she watched him cannibalize her love and make it part of him. Her heart belonged to him now. It would be his forever. The voices of the choir rose to fill every corner of the room as it reached another dizzying crescendo.

That's when Glenda looked around and saw the choir had now joined them in the room. Dozens of men and women, their eyes all glazed with that same fanatical gleam she knew must have been in her own. The outpouring of love that came from them was staggering. As her eyes slowly adjusted to the dark basement, she could see how beautiful Lord's vocalists were. The men were all smooth and sinuous, the women sensuous and curvaceous. All of them were naked, masturbating and caressing each other as their eyes gleamed with lust and fixed on Lord with adoration and hunger. They were each missing their hearts. A jagged hole ringed by savaged flesh and tissue was all that was left where their hearts should have been. That's when she figured out what it was about the song. It was not about giving your heart to God, it was about giving it to Lord. They were singing about him.

As she watched, Lord seemed to grow in her eyes until he filled the entire room and then the entire church. The walls of the church fell away and he continued to rise, to grow, to expand until he filled the night sky in all directions and blotted out the moon and stars. He was everything to her now. He was the world to her, and nothing would ever exist for her again but him. He was her new Higher Power.

The choir moved in to absorb her into their ranks. Their hands flew across her flesh, once again stirring her desire and bringing her to the brink of ecstasy. She began to sing. Her voice flew out of her like a spirit bound for heaven as tears of joy rolled down her face. She didn't need anyone to teach her the lyrics. It had been in her all along.

Lord smiled as their joyful noise filled him.

TORSO

She was just a torso.
No arms to hold me,
barely more
than bleeding stubs
amputated at the shoulder
No voluptuous hips
or sumptuous thighs
just jagged ivory shards
jutting forth from her pelvic bone.
No lips to kiss.
Barely more
than teeth
without tongue
or throat.
Yet still shrieking
and cursing
and shouting.
No breasts to suckle and caress,
just bony ribs
and the empty cavity
where her heart had been.

STAY IN
THE LINES

I had just purchased two new canes from an antique shop earlier that day, and I was busy cleaning them while Baby lay naked beside me on her belly, hugging her new stuffed doggie and coloring in *the Little Mermaid* coloring book I had bought for her the day before.

When I was done cleaning the canes, I stood and looked down at her lovely ass. Just looking at it caused a stirring in my pants. Such a beautiful ass. My bite marks were still visible on her hips, thighs, and each luscious buttock. Most of the other bruises I had given her the night before had already faded or yellowed. She needed some new ones. I began tapping the cane up and down her thighs and that sweet ass.

"That feels good. Should I stop coloring now?"

"No. Just stay in the lines."

I continued warming up her ass and thighs with the cane, and then I gave her the first hard lash with the cane that immediately raised a welt.

"Ow! Daddy!"

"Keep coloring."

She reached for another crayon, red for the shell of the crab she was working on.

I gave her another hard crack.

"Stay in the lines," I said firmly. "Make Daddy a pretty

picture."

"Yes, Daddy."

I gave her a few more hard licks, and she put her head down and began to shiver. I stepped out of my pants, removed my shirt, and picked up the cane again. I brought the cane down even harder, almost breaking skin. Her shivers increased. Dopamine rush. Subspace. She was riding an endorphin high now. Her ass and thighs were striped with welts, and I began filling in the spaces between the welts until the pale skin on my beautiful baby's ass was a red woven quilt of livid wounds.

My cock was harder than calculus. I stroked it, growling low in my throat, imagining cumming on her reddened ass cheeks. What a beautiful picture that would make.

Each time I brought the cane down on those luscious globes of succulent flesh, watched them wobble, heard my baby moan, my own engorged manhood throbbed in response. Her ass looked like something that belonged on a dessert tray.

My growls grew louder. The beast was fully awake and eager to mate. Baby had her head down again, crayon clutched in her fist, trembling from head to toe. I knew from experience just how wet her pussy was right now. The thought of her wetness deepened the growls. They were now a heavy bass rumble like the vibrations from cheap speakers when the bass and volume are turned up higher than they can handle. Only these speakers were blasting *Wild Kingdom*. The sound of some large predator preparing to take down an antelope.

I dropped the cane and laid down on top of her, easing my full length inside those lubricious folds of silken flesh, deep into her sex. I fucked her slow. All the way in, filling her up. She gasped.

"Keep coloring."

"Yes, Daddy."

Almost all the way out.

"Your cock feels so good!"

All the way in, even deeper this time.

I increased my rhythm, furiously pounding into her, my balls slapping against her ass.

"Oh, Daddy. Oooh, you feel so good."

"Finish my picture. And stay in the lines."

"Ooooooh. Yessssss, Daddy." It was a sibilant whisper, hissed between clenched teeth.

I raised up on my knuckles so I could look down at her lovely ass and watch my cock slide in and out of her as I pounded her into the mattress.

"Oh, God! You feel so fucking huge!"

And I was. My cock was so hard it felt like a fifth limb. She was coloring in a leaf with a green crayon when my jackhammering in and out of her caused the crayon to slip.

"I told you to stay in the lines. That's one more lick with the cane. Now keep coloring."

"Yes, Daddy. I'll try. I've never tried to color while being fucked before."

"Every time you go outside the lines, you get another licking from the cane."

"Yes, Daddy."

I lowered myself down on top of her again, bit the back of her neck, and increased my rhythm, fast and hard, like a teenager getting his first piece of pussy, recklessly racing toward orgasm. The crayon slipped again.

"That's another one. Stay in the lines. Keep coloring."

"Oh, Daddy! Oh god!"

Her eyes were closed. Her sex was a waterfall. Her pussy clenched my cock like a fist.

"Did you hear what Daddy said?"

She nodded as she reached a trembling hand toward the crayon box and grabbed a yellow crayon to finish the flowers.

"Yes, Daddy."

"Make. It. Pretty. For. Me!"

I punctuated each word with a hard thrust, angry strokes that drove her hips into the mattress and forced the air from her lungs.

"Oh! Yes, Daddy! I will! I'll make it pretty! God, your cock feels so good!"

She finished the flowers, the seaweed, the crab's shell, only making two more mistakes. Now she reached for the blue crayon to color in the little bubbles. This was going to be hard. I almost laughed.

I raised up on my knuckles, into a planking position, watching my cock slide in and out of her sopping wet pussy as I slammed down into her again and again, battering her sex as if all the treasures of earth and heaven lay beyond its walls, and all I had to do was dig through her to get to them.

Not one bubble was in the lines.

I pulled out. Stood up. Picked up the cane.

"I told you to stay in the lines. Now, how many do you get?"

She hesitated. She was still trembling, trying to catch her breath.

"How many?" I demanded.

"Four."

"Count them off."

I lashed the cane across her ass, laying an angry red welt right between two earlier ones.

"One," she whispered breathlessly.

I brought the cane down again, laying welt upon welt.

"Two."

I striped the back of her thighs.

"Three."

The final stroke was harder than all the rest. I raised the cane above my shoulder, and whipped it down across her ass in a vicious arc that brought a fresh round of shivers to my baby girl's elegant form.

Later, as I laid in bed, looking at the picture my baby colored for me while she swallowed my cock, practicing her rapidly developing deep-throating skills, I counted all the times she had gone out of the lines. There were twelve in all. I owed her eight more licks. I came with a roar that emptied me, filling her talented mouth with my seed, and I contemplated whether to let those last few mistakes slide. After all, it was a pretty picture, and she did make Daddy very happy. Decisions. Decisions. I guess she'll find out when I see her tonight.

SICKENING

You are Gorgeous to the point of lustful excess
A horrible exaggeration of comeliness
Irresistible
as thunder
Beauty
a pregnant tumor
breeding wildly in your cells
grimace quantities of sensuality
too expansive to be contained
by flesh or spirit
You are gross with it
hideously engorged
bloated
with a loveliness so profound
as to be oppressive
a weight
bending your features
into abominable perfection
Sensuousness bubbles up out of you
a sweet unctuousness
oozing from your pores
permeating your clothes
the air around you

pooling at your feet
thick and syrupy
and I would lap it from your toes
like a thirsty dog
lick it from your skin
to feel its heat
upon my tongue
rub it over my face
neck
chest
grinning
giggling
so
so pretty
Irresistible
as thunder.

"CUM FOR ME"

"Let me go, Sir," Suzanne pleaded. "Pleeeease! I'm going crazy, Sir. I haven't cum in six months. This is torture!"

Marcus laughed.

"You shouldn't have left then. Serves you right. You want to cum? Then you know where to come."

He hung up the phone.

Suzanne screamed in exasperation, pounding the floor with her fists, and then she dialed her former Master again.

"What?" he barked, answering the phone on the first ring, as if he knew she would be calling back, and, of course, he did know.

"Just say it. Just this one time, Sir. Pleeease! Just give me permission to cum, you evil fuck!"

"Fuck you, bitch!"

He hung up again.

Suzanne threw the phone against her bedroom wall, screaming and crying hysterically. In a tantrum, she hurled herself around the room, breaking everything she could get her hands on: the lamp by her bed, picture frames, perfume bottles. She swept everything off her bookshelf onto the floor and then collapsed beside the small mound of books, sobbing uncontrollably.

Before she'd met Sir Marcus, she'd been multi-orgasmic.

As she'd often joked, she could make herself cum anywhere, anytime, just by rubbing her thighs together. During sex, it was not uncommon for her to have twenty or thirty orgasms. But Sir Marcus had changed all of that their first night together.

He was fucking her hard from behind, smacking her ass, pulling her hair, and biting her shoulder while pounding his nine-inch cock against her cervix like he was trying to reenter the womb. When she'd cum, he began to strangle her, which only made the orgasm stronger.

"I didn't give you permission to cum. You wait right there."

"Yes, Sir," Suzanne replied, feeling vulnerable and confused. Still on her knees. Still trembling with the aftershocks of her orgasm. They had played together before, at parties. Scenes with whips, floggers, and rope, even some breath play where he would wrap her face in plastic wrap and watch as she struggled to breathe, strip it away just as she started to turn blue, watch her gasp for air, and then wrap her head again. It had been so intense. She'd felt so connected to him, literally trusting him with her life and he'd never violated that trust, always knowing just how far to push her, avoiding her hard limits and heeding her triggers. But this was the first time they'd ever been alone together, the first time they'd actually had sex.

Of course they'd negotiated ahead of time. Just like it was any other scene. And he'd told her that she wasn't allowed to have an orgasm unless he said so, but she'd never experimented with orgasm control before and had just assumed he'd been kidding. She had been wrong.

When her Sir returned, he was carrying a dragon's tail made of one long piece of black suede, twisted loosely like she used to do with wet towels when she was a cheerleader in high school and they would pop each other with them in the shower. This one ended in a metal handle covered in spikes.

"Don't move. You have to be punished now. You are *never* to cum until I give you permission to cum. You understand that?"

"Yes, Sir. I'm sorry, Sir. I couldn't help it though, Sir. Your cock felt so good. You were fucking me so hard."

"Then you should have waited for me to give you the command."

He cracked the dragon's tail across her ass. No warning. No warm-up. Suzanne gasped and tears welled in her eyes. It stung like a son of a bitch!

"You get ten licks. You count them off."

"Yes, Sir. That's one, Sir."

He let the dragon's tail fly again.

"Two, Sir."

Again.

"Three, Sir."

Again. This time it hit her on the hip and drew blood. She felt it trickle down her thigh. It wasn't the first time she'd been cut, but this was different somehow. This wasn't fun playtime. This was punishment. Still, even this was arousing the fuck out of her. Suzanne wanted so badly to touch herself. To make herself cum while her Sir whipped her bloody with the dragon's tail, but she knew that would only have gotten her into more trouble and worsened her punishment.

"Four, Sir!" she cried out.

When he reached ten, her new Master took his enormous cock in hand and eased it into her anus with only his saliva as lube. Suzanne grunted and groaned, a fresh flood of tears pouring from her eyes, as she was fucked hard in her ass. But the tears weren't from the beating or even from being sodomized. The tears were because she was on the verge of another orgasm, and she was doing everything she could to hold it at bay.

She felt her Sir's fingers slip inside her sopping wet pussy and she began to moan and whimper.

"Pleeeease, Sir. May I cum now?"

"No," he replied forcefully while he continued fucking her hard in the ass and began rubbing her engorged clitoris with his thumb while still fucking her wet pussy with two fingers.

Her legs were trembling. She felt like she was going to lose her mind if she had to wait another second. Then she felt her Master's already enormous cock swell even larger, felt his body tense and begin to jerk and hitch, and then the warm liquid eruption as he began to ejaculate in her asshole.

"Cum for me, now," he whispered, and Suzanne exploded. Orgasm tumbled down upon orgasm in an unending torrent that threatened to take her very sanity with it, crushing her beneath a tremendous avalanche of pleasure.

"Oh, god! What the fuck did you just do to me?" She was still cumming.

Sir Marcus pumped her asshole a few final exhausted thrusts, emptying the last of his seed deep in her bowels before withdrawing his cock.

He leaned down and grabbed her face in one large hand, forcing her to look him in his eyes.

"Are you my slave now?"

"Yes, Sir. Yes, Master."

"Then you cum when I tell you, and only when I tell you. Understand?"

"Yes, Sir, but...but what if you aren't here? I mean, what if I'm home alone and I want to masturbate or something?"

"Then you call me when you're close and you ask for permission to cum. Just like if I were here."

"But...what if you don't answer the phone?"

"That's my commitment to you. I'll always answer the phone when you call."

"But what if you can't? What if you're busy? Or what if you say no?"

Sir Marcus gave her a look that dried the saliva in her mouth and raised the hair on her arms and neck. Goosebumps rose all over her, and she shivered and immediately dropped her eyes and tried to look away, but her new Master forced her head back up.

"Look at me! If you can't get hold of me, and you don't get my permission, then you don't cum. Understand?"

Suzanne nodded in agreement.

"I want to hear you say it."

"I understand."

"You understand what?"

"I do not cum without your permission, Sir."

"Ever!"

"Yes, Sir. Not ever."

And so had begun her training.

After they had been together for a month, it got to the point where she no longer even needed to touch herself. His words alone were enough to bring her to climax.

"Cum for me."

And she would gush in her panties. Wherever. Whenever.

He would call her at work.

"Cum for me."

And she would orgasm, as silently as possible, right there in her cubicle. He had ordered her to call him in the middle of a company meeting once, and she had done as ordered, dialing his number just as the CEO stood up to speak.

"Cum for me."

And she had to bite her lip to keep from screaming as a powerful orgasm thundered through her. At a family dinner, as he sat beside her talking football with her father and flattering her mother with praise for her peach cobbler, he'd leaned over and whispered in her ear.

"Cum for me."

Her parents thought she'd had some kind of seizure. Her teenaged sister had stared at her suspiciously, eying the wet spot spreading in Suzanne's little white cotton shorts.

But then Suzanne had decided she wanted to play with other people. She had always considered herself polyamorous, and bisexual. So being with just one man, serving only one Master, despite how great the sex was, began to bore her. When she had spoken to her Master about it, he was less than receptive.

"You want another Master? You want pussy too. My dick isn't enough for you?"

"No, Sir. It isn't like that. I just...I just want to explore, try new things, and I've just never been with one person. Ever. I don't think it's my thing. I mean, I'm bi. I miss girls. I love your dick, Sir. It's the biggest, most beautiful cock I've ever seen, and I love the way you fuck me and how we play together, but I like pussy too. I just feel stifled, trapped."

"Then you're free. Go! Do what you want with whomever you want. I don't keep no slave that don't want to be kept."

"But...but you'll still be my Master, right? I'll still belong to you, right?"

In answer, Sir Marcus pulled up his pants and buckled them, then removed a small key from his pocket and turned Suzanne around.

"No! No, Master! Please! I'm sorry! I didn't mean it!"

He unlocked the tiny padlock on the little stainless steel collar around her neck and pulled it off her throat.

"No, Master! Please, Sir! Don't do this!"

Suzanne dropped to her knees, hugging her now ex-Master's shins with one arm and trying to reach out and grab her collar back with the other hand. Sir Marcus snatched it away from her and put it in his pocket.

She collapsed at his feet, kissing his shoes.

"I love you, Sir! I'm sorry! I don't need anyone else."

"Good-bye," he said, pulling his feet out of her grasp and walking to the door, leaving Suzanne sobbing on the floor, almost in the exact same spot where she was lying now, six months later, after just throwing a $500 smartphone against the wall.

No matter who she was with in the months that followed her break-up with Master—male, female, dom, sub, switch, vanilla, sadist, masochist—she could not have an orgasm. It was like she was dead from the waist down. Where she used to be able to cum with very little stimulation, now she couldn't cum even with the most talented tongue making mouth-music against her clit for an hour while being fucked by the biggest, fattest cock she could find. Nothing worked. She still needed her Master's permission to cum. He had never released her. He had never given the power back to her, and she didn't know how to take it back.

Suzanne stood up and wiped the tears from her eyes, leaving a black smear on the back of her hand as her mascara came off with it. She used her T-shirt to wipe off the snot and saliva drooling from her mouth and nose. She was pathetic. This was how her former Master had wanted her. Reduced to nothing. He was a true sadist...and not in a good way. There was nothing consensual about what he was doing to her now, torturing her for his own sadistic pleasure.

After throwing her T-shirt into the laundry and getting a fresh one, and then changing into a pair of jeans and sneakers, Suzanne left her apartment for the first time in days. She'd spent the last seventy-two hours furiously masturbating with a dildo, a Hitachi, and the vibrator with the little bunny on the top with the long silicone tongue. Her vagina felt sore and raw and she still hadn't cum. Worse yet, she had pulled a "no-call, no-show" at work, which probably meant the end of her employment there. And, no matter what the government said about an "economic recovery," finding a new job was going to be a bitch.

"That piece of shit ruined my life! How could he do this to me?"

She left her little one-bedroom apartment, locking the door. Her destination was never in doubt; what she would do when she got there was still coalescing slowly in her mind.

She parked her little red Rav 4 in the driveway of her former master's home. His lawn was well manicured, shrubs trimmed—there were even flowers in the planters. She knew better than to think he'd done any of this himself. He had a new slave, a service slave who liked to garden. She felt a twinge of jealousy.

"That bastard."

She didn't know why she felt this sudden flash of anger. He wasn't her Master anymore. She had moved on. But she hadn't meant for it to mean the end of their relationship. That was his choice. He had abandoned her and left her with this curse as a final punishment.

She walked up the walkway, wondering if Sir Marcus would suddenly fling open the door and greet her with righteous anger, drag her into the house, punish her good, make her bruise and bleed, debase and degrade her, force her to do all manner of disgusting things, ass-to-mouth, piss on her, make her lick his hairy asshole, and then fuck her hard and say those three words she'd been begging to hear for six months.

But no one came to meet her as she walked up his driveway. She knocked on the door. Waited. Then rang the doorbell.

His dented old silver Lexus wasn't in the driveway, but he might have parked it in the garage. There were no other cars around. So if Sir Marcus was home, at least that meant he was probably alone.

After a few long moments, the door creaked open. Sir Marcus stood before her in his bathrobe, squinting against the afternoon sun. His eyes were bloodshot, his wooly hair nappy and uncombed. His lips were dry and ashen. He'd gained weight, and his paunch poked out from the open robe. This was not the Master she remembered. He looked like a old drunk.

"Bitch, what the hell do you want? What the fuck are you doing here?"

She slowly raised the little pink Smith & Wesson .38 he'd bought her for her birthday what felt like a lifetime ago.

"Fuck are you going to do with that? Bitch, you think you scare me? I'm your Master. You ain't mine."

"You took my collar off, remember? You're not my Master anymore."

He stepped forward. The barrel of the gun poked him in the center of his chest.

"I'll always be your Master."

He touched his finger to her temple.

"I'm up here. I'll always be in your head. You can't get me out."

"Let me go, Marcus." She didn't feel right calling this shadow of her former Master "Sir."

"I ain't never letting you go," he said, reaching around to palm her ass and pull her closer, heedless of the gun jammed against his chest. "I own this ass and I always will."

"You don't own shit, Marcus!"

"Oh, yeah? Cum for me."

The gun slipped from her hand as the orgasm struck her like a bolt of lightning thrown by the hand of God. Her legs buckled, and she dropped to her knees. Waves of pleasure crashed through her nervous system, turning her sex into an open faucet.

"Oh, god! Oh, thank you, Sir! Thank you!"

"See?" he said, looming above her as she continued to jerk and convulse with the residual tremors from her cataclysmic climax. "I told your ass, I own you. You'll always be mine. Cum for me."

Another orgasm ripped through her, doubling her over. She curled into the fetal position as it boomed up from between her legs like the crescendo of a thousand orchestras playing at once.

"Cum for me," he said again, and the next orgasm wracked her already convulsing form. These were more powerful than the orgasms she had during normal sex, the little ones that came in wave after wave. Each of these felt apocalyptic, like the world was flying asunder all around her. It felt like she was dying.

"Stop," she begged. "That's enough."

"Cum for me," he whispered again, grinning down at her with that smug, superior expression. Another orgasm came barreling through her, bringing pulsating waves of pleasure more agonizing than any pain she'd ever experienced at his hands or any others.

He was still smiling down at her triumphantly as she convulsed helplessly on the floor. She could see his lips forming the words, see his tongue press against the roof of his mouth to form the first syllable.

That's when she pulled the trigger.

She didn't remember picking up the gun again, had no idea how it had gotten back in her hand, why Marcus hadn't kicked it away or picked it up himself. Such hubris. He thought he could control every-fucking-thing. Too convinced of his own power to fear even a crazy, desperate woman with a gun. He seemed to fall forever. The hole blossomed in the center of his chest, and red erupted from the wound, timed almost perfectly with her final orgasm, before he landed beside her, dead the instant his head struck the concrete walkway.

"I'm free," Suzanne whispered.

And you'll never cum again, something deep inside her mind whispered back. She looked down at the gun in her hand and knew she had no other choice if she really wanted to be free of her Master forever. She put the barrel between her teeth. It was still hot and tasted of sulfur. Just before she pulled the trigger, she felt a feint yet familiar stirring in her loins that began to build to a thunderous climax.

Well I'll be damned, she thought, and then all thoughts ceased.

SEXXXY

My life was a model of moderation until I saw her that day. There was almost nothing obviously attractive about her, to my tastes, yet almost everything about her was dripping with raw, carnal sexuality. She was riding a motorcycle while wearing a red latex miniskirt. The skirt was hiked up so high on her thick thighs, I could see the wonderful results of a recent Brazilian wax. Almost immediately, the self-discipline I'd worked so hard to cultivate began to slip.

Some might have called my myriad paranoias a fear of the unknown, of new experiences. Many would have just called me a pussy. In truth, I was terrified of losing control, afraid to find myself carried away by passions I could not bend to my will and master with reason. It was one of the main reasons I had remained a bachelor for so long. Women found me boring. I didn't drink or use drugs or play video games or hang out in nightclubs. I wasn't very experimental in the bedroom. My last girlfriend jokingly referred to me as "The Missionary Man" because of my reluctance to try new sexual positions.

I didn't even drink coffee or smoke cigarettes because of my overwhelming fear of addictions. I panicked if I had an energy drink two days in a row, afraid I was growing addicted to fructose and guarana. I had never even watched a pornographic movie, having heard of people succumbing to the lure of Internet porn and wasting hours in front of the computer screen, jacking off until their cocks bled. Addictions led to dangerous excesses. People loss jobs, stole, and got themselves incarcerated, shunned, and scorned by polite society because of excesses. But from the moment I spotted the girl in the miniskirt, I knew I would follow her down the road to excess. Everything about her screamed wantonness and overindulgence.

She straddled the custom motorcycle like a lover. A coy smile teased the corners of her lips as she throttled the engine, and the bike roared between her thighs. It was a Harley Davidson, wide and low with tall handlebars like a chopper and a large seat. It was painted black, purple, and red with skulls and flames and chrome pipes that looked like bones. I only glanced at the bike briefly. My attention was quickly torn away by the voluptuous woman who rode it.

My underwear felt uncomfortably tight as I stared into my side mirror and straight up her skirt. She seemed to spread her legs wider, inviting my eyes into the dark place between them. I was so transfixed by that hairless cleft, I didn't see the light change until the cars behind me began to honk and she cruised past me and winked.

I couldn't tell you what it was about her I found so attractive, besides her obvious lack of shame. She was large everywhere. Not just fat, though she was obviously carrying quite a bit of excess adipose tissue. She was more than six feet tall and had wide shoulders and muscular arms like a bodybuilder's. Her triceps flexed and rippled as she worked the throttle. Her legs were titanic. Her calves bulged like biceps, and her quadriceps, like the rest of her, were an intimidating combination of fat and muscle. She had breasts that stuck out two feet off her chest but barely jiggled thanks to a bra reinforced with steel mesh. She had a large stomach but her breasts stuck out twice as far as her gut, which effectively hid it unless you were obsessed with such things, which I usually was.

I had never been into large women. Fat people actually disgusted me a little. Obesity had always seemed to me like the living epitome of excess, greed, lack of willpower and control, of laziness. I preferred thin or athletic women. But her thick muscular frame challenged all my prejudices. The muscles in her arms and legs made it clear that she was not lazy. You didn't get triceps like that sitting on a couch eating ice cream. It took willpower and discipline. Still, she definitely was not missing any meals.

Looking at the large woman's sexually extravagant proportions, I felt the most powerful, overwhelming lust I'd felt since puberty. It startled and frightened me more than a little. I squirmed uncomfortably in my chair. My erection jabbed at my stomach, bent backward by my tighty-whities.

The woman had beautiful red hair that hung down her back and blew in the wind as she rode. Her eyes were a fiery emerald green, and her lips were full and plump, painted a brazen red, and I knew her. I was certain of it. I had gone to high school with her back in Philadelphia. Her name was Katrina.

What the hell was she doing in San Francisco?

In high school she had been one of those tragically pretty fat girls that skinny girls teased mercilessly who either became a slut, a fag-hag, or a suicidal introvert. As I recalled, she had been the suicidal type. She used to wear dark clothes and white makeup with black lipstick, eye shadow, and nail polish, and would sit in the hallways reading Anne Rice, Henry Miller, and Anaïs Nin, quoting Emily Dickinson and Sylvia Plath, and listening to The Cure and Depeche Mode. I barely noticed her then. I had my own problems. She was a social outcast, and though I was not exactly part of the "in-crowd," I could have been if my interests hadn't tended toward the nerdy. Chess club, Dungeons and Dragons, Tolkien, Isaac Asimov, Stephen King, and Douglas Adams novels were my life then. I worked out incessantly and had the hard body and chiseled good looks that girls went for, but I was too conservative and introverted even then. Girls found me weird. There were rumors I was a homosexual. The rumors were how I met Jason, who quickly became my best friend. He was gay and had tried to pick me up one day after school. I was too embarrassed to tell him I wasn't gay and let him kiss me.

The next day he came up to me in the hallway between classes.

"You're not gay, are you?"

I shook my head.

"Then why'd you let me kiss you?"

I shrugged.

He laughed, and we started hanging out, and the teasing increased.

Jason was the one who encouraged me to join the chess team and the creative writing club and introduced me to his D&D group. I was still fending off aggressive recruitment from the football and basketball coaches. I told them I'd never even watched organized sports and found them boring and barbaric. I only worked out because I lived in a bad neighborhood and having big muscles was an easier way to avoid becoming a crime victim than carrying a gun or joining a gang. Finally they stopped bothering me about it. They would pass me in the halls and give me looks of pity and disgust. Their expressions said, "What a waste." I knew they were right, but I liked what I liked and that was Jason and D&D and my chess club buddies.

Throughout high school, I avoided the wild high school parties because there were drugs and alcohol there, and I hated the smell of cigarette smoke and weed. I was known as

Lionel Burger, the good-looking geek. That put me one rung above Katrina McClory, the emo devil slut, on the school social ladder.

She rode along next to me for several blocks. I wondered what she would have thought of me now, thirty-four and single, driving a Toyota Prius and working as an editor at a weekly newspaper. She had blossomed into some sort of badass body-building she-devil, while I remained the good-looking geek.

She turned the corner from Market Street onto Haight Street, and I found myself turning the corner to follow her. I hadn't decided to do it. I was on autopilot.

I followed her as she drove up Haight Street to the Lower Haight and parked in front of a coffee shop on the corner of Haight and Church. I parked directly in front of the place and watched her as she sat down and drank some sort of coffee that was covered in whipped cream and drizzled with chocolate. She was reading a magazine that seemed to be about latex fetishes with a cover that was almost pornographic. Somehow, despite her outfit and salacious choice in periodicals, she did not appear brazen or shameless so much as free. She looked completely free. I envied her.

I sat there watching her for more than an hour. I watched her snatch up her smartphone when it had apparently rang or received a text message or an alert or something. She pressed a few buttons, smiled, and then snatched up her things and hurried out of the shop. Curious, I followed.

She left her bike parked in front of the coffee shop and hurried down the street, staring at her smartphone like it was receiving some sort of signal and she was following it. I had read about smartphone apps that would alert you when someone you knew was nearby. There were even dating apps that told you if another single user who was compatible with you was in the vicinity.

She reached an unmarked storefront with blacked-out windows, rang the doorbell, and then ducked inside. My curiosity was now on overdrive.

I climbed out from behind the wheel of the Prius and followed her. There was a little silver plaque, about the size of a credit card, just above the doorbell. The plaque said "Halloween's." I rang the doorbell.

A man covered in tattoos opened the door.

"You by yourself?"

I nodded.

"Then it's thirty bucks."

I paid the thirty bucks, not knowing what I'd just purchased. *A service? Some sort of experience?*

I tentatively stepped inside a dark room that reeked of a strong disinfectant that was still not quite strong enough to mask the smell of blood and semen. Every instinct within me, primal flight-or-fight reflexes reacting to the smell of violence, told me to "Run! Flee! Save yourself before it's too late!"

Then I spotted Katrina walking down a long hallway with black walls and I followed. There were closed doors on either side of the hallway. Loud music blared from the speakers with bass so heavy it made my chest hurt. It had a driving techno beat and was full of moans and screams. It took me a moment to realize the moans and screams were not coming from the speakers. They were coming from all around me.

What the hell is this place?

Ahead of me, still staring at her cell phone, Katrina disappeared into one of the rooms. I crept tentatively toward the open doorway and paused, trembling. I took several deep breaths, looked back down the hallway at the door I'd just come through, closed my eyes, and prayed for guidance. As always, God, the cosmos, the life force, or whatever it was that people prayed to was silent. I didn't expect anything more.

Praying was more of a habit left over from my devout Baptist parents. I tended to believe in the empirically verifiable.

The chills racing up and down my spine and the trembling in my legs decided the matter for me. I turned to walk back the way I'd come. Then I heard Katrina's voice. It sounded angry. Then another voice, deep and husky, moaning. I turned back through the door, which was still slightly cracked, as if she had known I was following and was inviting me to join her. I peered inside.

I don't know what I expected to see, some sort of orgy, an S&M scene, male prostitutes, whatever expectations I had before peering through that crack in the door shattered like a pane of glass in a hurricane when I saw the massive man, larger and more muscular even than Katrina, lying face down on a metal operating table with his wrists and ankles shackled to each corner, while Katrina knelt above him, anally raping him with a strap-on dildo that looked more like an elephant tusk than a phallus. It was curved and pointy, the length and girth of a child's arm, at least two-feet long, and appeared to have been fashioned from ivory. The man had a leather hood over his head, and Katrina had apparently put duct tape over the tiny zippered mouth-slit and the two nose holes. The husky moans I'd heard from outside were his muffled screams. He was suffocating even as Katrina made a ruin of his lower intestines. Blood and lacerated hemorrhoidal tissue now covered the dildo/tusk. Katrina was thrusting with all her might, sweating profusely from the exertion. As she drove her hips and pelvis down into the man's muscular gluteus maximus, pile-driving the lethal sex-toy deep into the helpless bodybuilder, obliterating his rectum, coring it out with a hideous ripping, squishing sound, like someone juicing an orange.

When she finally withdrew the ivory phallus from the bleeding ruin that was once an anus, half the man's intestinal track appeared to come with it, along with an avalanche of blood and feces, erupting from his asshole like a volcano. My stomach revolted. I fell to my knees, vomiting uncontrollably.

Katrina watched me, smiling with amusement while she unstrapped the dildo. She pulled out some wet naps and wiped smears of blood and feces from her thighs, doing the same to the dildo before tucking the thing back inside a huge purse she carried with her. I was still doubled over in the hallway. She stepped over me, slammed the door behind her, and then knelt and lifted me to my feet with all the effort one might use to heft a Chihuahua into a Prada handbag.

"Let's go, Lionel," she whispered and hurried me toward the front door. The guy who'd let me in and took my money was stomping down the hall toward us in long purposeful strides. *She knew my name, knew who I was. How?*

"Did you just fucking throw up in here? Is that your vomit on my fucking floor? Jesus Christ! That smells terrible! You expect me to clean that shit up for you?"

What he was smelling was likely what had boiled up out of the dead man's rectum rather than the pound of liquefied vegan offal I had just regurgitated. Together we raced out the door, past my little blue Prius, and hopped onto her tricked-out Harley.

"How did you know my name? Where are we going?"

I know. It was weird that those were the first questions to come to mind after watching her murder some guy built like a pro-wrestler by sodomizing him with a strap-on straight out of *Lair of the White Worm.* But I was afraid to ask about that. I was trying to put the whole thing out of my mind, trying to dismiss the possibility that I might be next. Because I still wanted to know her. More now than ever. I was terrified, mortally afraid, but the thought of never knowing why she'd done what she did, what else she was capable of, how she knew my name, and, most importantly, who this beautiful, seductive Zaftig murderess was would have been unbearable.

She looked over her shoulder at me and smiled as she gunned the engine. The smile held the promise of pleasure, the threat of pain.

"Hold on."

I pulled her close. She smelled like jasmine and roses and beer and cigarettes and sweat and sex and blood.

"How do you know my name?"

"I remember you, Lionel. I never forgot you. I never forgot any of you."

She turned the corner, leaving Haight Street and gunning it down Church Street, headed toward the Castro District.

"Where are we going?"

She laughed.

"Lionel?"

"Y-yes?"

"You still haven't asked me why I killed that guy back there."

"I-I figured that was your own personal business. I mean, it-it's none of my business."

"Well, if you're going to be hanging with me, then my business is your business, right?"

I didn't know what to say. Katrina was grinding her sizable ass against my crotch, which was responding with an erection that felt like it had drained half the blood from my brain.

"So, what-what's your business? I mean, if you don't mind my asking."

"I kill people."

All the saliva dried up in my mouth. She said it so callously, so cavalierly, without the slightest hint of remorse.

"For money?"

"Sometimes."

"Was that for money? I mean, what you did to that guy. Did someone pay you for that?"

"Yeah. He did."

That made my mind spin. *Someone paid her to fuck him to death with a dildo made out of an elephant tusk?*

"Why would he...why would anyone pay for something like that?"

"It was his fantasy," she replied with a shrug. "He had a fetish for dildos."

And that explained it for her. That was all she needed to know in order to rip a man's guts out through his asshole.

"You heard about that guy in Germany who met a man on the Internet and let the guy eat him alive?"

I nodded.

"And that guy who killed himself by letting himself get fucked in the ass by a horse? He filmed the whole thing. I have a copy of it. It's pretty sick."

I nodded. Of course she had a copy of it. Still, I could not imagine getting ass-raped by a Clydesdale being any sicker than having your insides ruptured by a twenty-four-inch piece of ivory.

"So where are we going now?"

"To see another client."

"How do you find them? I mean, how do they find you?"

She handed me her cell phone. There were picture of men and woman from age twenty to ninety complete with phone numbers and e-mail and physical addresses. Above it were the words "fuck me to death."

"It's a new app."

"What's it called?"

"*Eros Morte.*"

"Sex Death?"

She looked over her shoulder at me and smiled.

"And this app does what? It finds people who want to be fucked to death?"

She nodded. The whole thing sounded completely insane.

I had a lot of questions, a lot of fears. I wanted to hop off the bike and run for my life, the same way I felt standing out in that hallway, listening to that big guy grunt and moan while Katrina rode him. But I was curious. This was so much more than the horrors I had imagined I would find in drugs or Internet porn. This was completely over-the-rainbow.

"Why would anyone want to die like that?" I asked. My voice had a desperate squeak, like the timid voice of a bullied child.

This time she didn't turn around. She shouted her reply into the wind, over the ferocious roar of the Harley's 1,340 cc v-twin engine, and it blew back into my face like the flaming ash and embers from a forest fire, yet instead of burning my eyes, her words burned away at the last sane notions of morality and humanity I was clinging to.

"Most people live unremarkable lives. At the end, they want a remarkable death. If no one remembers anything else about 'em, they'll fucking remember what I did to 'em! Jack the Ripper murdered prostitutes in the dregs of England, people who lived and died in relative obscurity. But he immortalized them when he carved those women up. Their stories have been retold in countless books and movies. Would anyone have ever heard of those women had they not been his victims? Do you think anyone would still be talking about 'em? Even their own families? The only reason their names are not lost to history is because of how they were butchered. Well, that's what that guy wanted. That's what they all want. The notoriety that can only come from a truly spectacular end. Of course, some of them are just kinky fuckers, masochists looking to get off one last time before they die. And that's cool too. It's not my place to knock anyone's kink. I'm more than a little kinky myself, in case you hadn't noticed."

She winked at me, and that mundane gesture juxtaposed with such an alien explanation for torture and murder was almost too much. This was all so surreal, so impossible. My brain was having trouble reconciling the dissonance between all I thought I knew about humanity and this sudden influx of new information that utterly contradicted it all on the most basic, existential level. The one thing I'd always believed it was safe to conclude about all living organisms was that they naturally moved from pain and toward pleasure, from self-annihilation toward self-preservation, except under the most dire of circumstances. And even the suicidal did not purposely seek an extraordinarily painful end. They wanted something quick and painless. Not...*this*. Yet what she'd said made sense to me somehow, and that was the most terrifying thing of all.

"What does this next client want you to do to him?"

"Her. And you'll see. You wouldn't want me to ruin the surprise, would you?"

Even with her back to me, I could hear the smile in her voice.

We pulled up outside an apartment building overlooking Market Street. Market Street was packed, as it always was. Well-groomed, athletically built men in tight blue jeans and tight, plain white T-shirts paraded up and down the street amid the businessmen in shirts and ties, middle-aged men in brightly colored polo shirts, hipsters, hip-hoppers, and leathermen. Similarly dressed women were interspersed with the men along with several large women in work boots, overalls, and wife-beaters. I had always avoided this part of town with its elicit bars and nightclubs and men in ass-less chaps. Now I was excited by it. I knew Katrina was about to show me a side of the Castro I would have never been able to discover on my own, maybe a side I would one day wish I had never discovered.

Knowing Katrina's next "client" was a woman sent my mind down dark paths, imagining acts of horrific debauchery

I would never have let myself entertain had I not seen what I had in Halloween's. Was she going to use that ivory dildo on a woman? I was surprised that the thought excited me as much as it horrified, but then, I was imagining a woman built like a supermodel, not the aging mass of plastic surgery scars that greeted us on the top floor of the apartment building.

Despite what must have been a dozen different plastic surgeries, her face clearly marked her age as somewhere in her sixties, but her body had been remarkably well preserved. She had huge fake breasts and an ass that had obviously undergone a Brazilian butt lift. It would have been lovely taken on its own, but attached to those over-tanned, wrinkled, emaciated thighs, they looked like the bags of silicone they were, as did her enormous mammaries.

She was completely nude when she opened the door. Her face was so tanned it was a burnt orange, like fried bologna. And her lips had so much collagen in them they resembled two fat red slugs slithering across her mouth. Numerous facelifts had pulled her eyebrows nearly up to her hairline, and her nose was almost nonexistent, just two slits in her face. I stifled a scream, horrified by the hideousness of it all. With all the work she'd had done, I guessed she was probably closer to eighty than sixty.

The woman regarded me casually, and then turned and walked back into the apartment, heading for her bedroom. We followed, closing the front door behind us.

The apartment was like nothing I could ever have imagined. Granite countertops and marble tiles in a kitchen stocked with oversized, stainless steel appliances, dark-cherry raised-panel cabinets, and dark-cherry hardwood floors covered everywhere else in the apartment. All the light fixtures and door hardware were a dark, oil-rubbed bronze that matched the wood floors. There were huge paintings on the walls lit with track lighting, clearly originals, though I couldn't place the artist. Abstract swirls of red, pink, and tan reminiscent of Francis Bacon yet more lascivious. I could make out a breast, an ass, a vagina, a penis, and teeth in the splashes of red dripping down the canvas. The signature on the bottom of the piece nearest me said "Joseph Miles." The name seemed vaguely familiar, but I had barely passed my art history course in college. I had only taken it because I thought it would be easier than world history.

I was so preoccupied with the painting and the overall beauty of the woman's apartment that I didn't notice the large zippered pouch Katrina withdrew from the big handbag she carried. Not until I followed her into the bedroom and she opened it up and laid its contents on the floor beside the bed: knives, scalpels, pliers, and bone saws.

I looked from Katrina to the woman, who lay on the king-sized bed atop a sheet of ten millimeter plastic. She was in the process of self-medicating, jabbing a hypodermic needle into one of the thick, blue veins in her thighs. Her eyes rolled skyward almost immediately; the eyelids drooped. Every muscle in her body visibly relaxed, and a smile crossed her face. Heroine, or something very much like it, I imagined. Though all I knew of such drugs was what I'd read in books or seen in movies. I had never witnessed anyone get high before.

"I'm ready," she said.

And Katrina went to work.

I watched in horror as the massive woman took a scalpel to the old lady's lips, slowly slicing them off her face, leaving only her brilliantly white teeth (obviously capped) beaming out from that burnt-orange face. But Katrina didn't leave her those either. She picked up the pliers and plucked the woman's teeth, one by one, from her mouth. The woman moaned and grunted but never screamed. Even when Katrina picked up one of the knives, straddled the woman's chest, and began carving on her face, the old woman never screamed. I watched in horror as she lopped off the old lady's ludicrously small nose.

Katrina reached out and rubbed the woman's oversized breasts, tweaking the nipples a bit. Then she leaned down and sucked each one until the nipples were fully erect. She snaked her hand down the old woman's liposuctioned abs, down between her blue-veined thighs, and eased one finger then another and another into the woman's hairless snatch. With her thumb, she rubbed the old woman's clitoris.

Katrina was remarkably deft in the art of pleasure. Easily as talented in this skill as she was at torture and murder. What little I knew about female anatomy told me orgasm should have been impossible for the old woman at this point, yet the woman's body began to respond, despite the immense pain she must have been in.

"Fuck her, Lionel."

"Wh-what? Did you just say fuck her?"

"Yeah. I can't get her off and cut her tit off at the same time. I need help, and since you're here ... you're going to pitch in. Take your cock out and stick it in her. It'll make the cutting hurt less. Unless you want to take the knife?"

"What? N-no. But I can't-I can't fuck her with half her face missing."

"Sure you can."

She stood up, and I took an involuntary step back. She sensed my fear and placed the knife back on the floor as she walked over to me. I relaxed only slightly. She reached out and grabbed hold of my cock, which hardened in her grasp. She stroked it through my jeans, and it had been so long since a woman had touched me like that, I nearly ejaculated in my shorts. She unzipped my pants, reached inside, pulled my underwear down and my penis out, and continued to stroke it, licking her palm and rubbing it over the head.

"Fuck her, Lionel."

"I-I can't."

"Fuck her, Lionel."

I shook my head.

She knelt down and licked the head of my cock and then sucked the whole thing down her throat. I felt like I would explode. I'd never felt anything like what her tongue was doing, swirling around my tumescent flesh, even as her lips were buried in my pubic hair with my cock pressing against her tonsils.

She slowly pulled my cock out of her mouth, teasing the underside of it with her tongue as it inched out of her throat.

"Do you want to fuck me, Lionel?"

I nodded enthusiastically, emphatically. Yes, I wanted to fuck her. More than I could ever remember wanting anything or anyone in my life, I wanted to mount this crazy, homicidal obese woman with breasts larger than my head. I wanted to know all the dark and terrible erotic secrets she knew.

"Then fuck her first, Lionel. Pleeeease?"

I nodded, and Katrina pulled down my pants and underwear and led me over to the bed by my cock, still stroking it to keep it erect. The old woman was surprisingly moist. She was aroused despite her injuries.

"Fuck her hard, Lionel! Fuck her like you want to fuck me!"

I closed my eyes and imagined Katrina's titanic thighs wrapped around my back instead of this bleeding septuagenarian with half a face. I pounded my throbbing erection deep into the old crone's withered cooze, fucking her violently, the way Katrina had fucked the muscular guy at Halloween's. I kept my eyes closed, even when the screaming started and that wet, ripping, tearing sound as Katrina sawed the woman's breasts off her ribcage.

"Wait. I need to flip her over."

I pulled out and tried to keep my eyes shut tight as Katrina dumped the woman's breasts into a bucket beside the bed.

"Did you cum?"

I shook my head.

"I still need to cut her ass off, but you can fuck me while I do it if you want? I'd hate to leave you all blue-balled."

I waved her off.

"That's okay. I'll wait. Is it okay if I use the shower?"

Katrina chuckled, probably realizing my eyes were still shut.

"Sure. The bathroom is behind you."

I walked into the bathroom, still thinking about what Katrina'd done to the old woman, what I'd done. I'd been close to orgasm when Katrina told me to stop so she could turn the old woman over. If not for that, I'd have come in that half-dead old bag while Katrina unmade her. My erection never diminished even as I scrubbed myself vigorously, trying to wash the smell of sex off along with the memory of it. But the memory was not unpleasant. No matter how much I scolded myself for it, no matter how loudly my Christian moral conscience protested, I had enjoyed it immensely.

I stepped out of the shower and walked naked back into the bedroom. Katrina was naked, waiting for me beside the ruined corpse of the old woman. Her enormous breasts flopped down over an equally enormous belly with pink nipples the size of 9mm bullets. Katrina's thick muscular thighs were spread wide and she was fingering her clit, swollen to the size of a small grape, with one hand and finger fucking the old woman with the other. The woman was face down and her ass was gone; her coccyx and pelvic bone showed through where her buttocks had been. Katrina had undone all the work the surgeons had done over the years. It was then that I realized the woman was still alive.

Katrina smiled as she noted my erection.

"I always thought you were hot, Lionel. Even back in high school. Do you think I'm sexy, Lionel?"

I nodded slowly, eyes fixed on her rolls of naked flesh, taking it all in.

"You are so, so sexy!" I said.

"You ready to fuck me now?"

I was practically drooling on myself. My cock was so hard it felt like the skin was about to rip. I wanted to lick, suck, fuck, and cum on every inch of her.

"Do you have anything left for her? She *is* paying for this. Don't you think she deserves one last good fuck?"

I nodded again, and then walked over and Katrina licked the head of my cock once more, lubricating it before guiding me onto the old woman. I fucked that ancient, half-dead crone in the ass. My hips struck naked, blood-spattered bone with each thrust as I pounded into the old woman's rectum.

I spent the night alternating between fucking the old woman and fucking Katrina. One moment I was fucking the old woman in the ass, the next sliding my cock between Katrina's mammoth tits. I fucked the old woman's toothless mouth as Katrina rimmed my asshole with her tongue. The old woman perished, drowning in my semen, but she remained part of our threesome. Katrina cut off the woman's head and urged me to fuck it while she fisted me. Katrina licked the decapitated woman's pussy while I fucked the leather and latex-clad murderess in her rotund posterior. I came again and again. Five orgasms in all before we left the dead woman's apartment.

I felt like my life had ended. I had descended into hell. I had entered the inferno and mated with demons. I felt as disconnected from the rest of humanity as man was to a spider monkey. How could I face anyone after seeing the things I'd seen, doing what I had done?

Katrina drove me back to my car. I held her tight and

wept onto her back. She was the only one who would ever understand me now.

"Will I ever see you again?" I asked, sounding like a lost puppy.

Katrina smiled and ran her fingers through my hair, placing a long bloody kiss on my lips.

"You will if you want to. Do you know how you want to die?"

"I don't know," I answered. "Something sexy."

"I'll think of something," she said and winked.

UNTIL THE NEXT TIME

Filthy blood-drenched dreams
Writhing in rapturous pain
From cum-stained nightmares
I awaken with a howl
That silences her

Her corpse beside me
His vivisected remains
scattered everywhere
Meat, blood, condoms, and roses
His dead eyes watch us

He took her from me
I took them both to hell
One victim. One lover.
Vengeance and lust consumed them.

Silence creeps like rot
building dark walls between us
imprisoning me
leaving me alone again
until the next time.

THE WHOLE DAMN BAG

"I'm going to use every toy in my bag tonight, Baby."

She smiles at me. The way you smile at a child who tells you he's going to be a superhero when he grows up.

"No you won't. You'll use two or three toys, and then, as soon as I start squirming, you'll go all primal and attack me."

"Are you trying to say I can't control myself?"

"It's okay, Daddy. I love how we play."

"But you don't think I can control myself long enough to make it through the whole bag?"

She smiles and shakes her head.

"Uh-uh."

"I just wrote a whole post on control. It got like a thousand loves on Fetlife. I know what control is."

"I'm not saying you would ever hurt me."

"But you don't think I can control myself long enough to use all the toys?"

"Daddy, it's okay. "

"No. We're doing this! Get in the bedroom!"

"Ooookay," she says in that sing-song voice she uses when she's just humoring me.

I'll show her control. I'm the goddamn master of control! Is she getting in the shower? Damn, I love how her skin smells when she gets out of the shower.

I walk into the closet and drag the bag out into the bedroom. It's on wheels, so it rolls smoothly. I used to make fun of Doms with rolling suitcases filled with toys, yet here I am.

Note to self: don't judge people.

I unzip the bag and look inside.

Damn. There's a lot of shit in here! What the hell is a doing with so many fucking toys? No wonder I never use them all. I should sell some of this shit. Oh, here she comes.

She walks into the room. Almost glides, like some ethereal being, leaving the scent of wet skin and hair, bath soap, and her own lust, trailing in the air in her wake as she slips past me and spreads herself out on the sheets. She is... sSo. Fucking. Beautiful.

I tell her so. She smiles.

"Thank you, Daddy. I love when you tell me that."

She parts her legs, and I want so badly to bury my face between them, to cannibalize her sex, chew up into her uterus.

Control, brother. Control.

I take a deep breath.

Okay. I got this.

I sit beside her and begin rubbing her legs, her hips, her belly, her back. I squeeze her ass. Hard. Harder. I growl.

Oh shit. I'm losing it. Control. Get it under control.

I sniff her hair. Nuzzle her neck and cheek. I give her a playful nip on her shoulder. I tug at her skin a little with my teeth. Not too hard. I'm still holding it together. She begins stroking my cock. The growl rumbles up from the core of my being, down where the monster lives. And it is hungry. So hungry. She smells so good. Like fresh pastry. Or maybe that's just the monster, distorting my senses. All I know is I want to devour her.

"I love you so much. If you died right now, I'd eat your beautiful corpse."

She giggles.

"Only you could make cannibalism sound romantic. "

I push her down onto the bed. Roll her over. Her ass is so lovely. I want to bite it. I lean down and press my face against those succulent globes of flesh. So soft and warm. I rub my cheek against them, rub my lips, my forehead, the top of my head. I'm really growling now. It is one, long, continuous sound, like the purr of a lion. She feels so good. Smells so good. I want to rip her apart and taste her soul.

Whoa. Pull it together.

I sit up.

God. That is one lovely ass. I smack it. It wobbles salaciously, and everything starts to cloud over. I can feel my consciousness slipping away, the beast taking control. Lust, appetite, aggression. I spank her ass again, alternating between hard smacks and light ones, warming her up. I lean down and bite her, I thrash back and forth, tearing at her flesh. She tries to wriggle away from me, but I pin her down, biting her hips and thighs. I bite her ribs, just under her arm, and she yelps. It is a wonderful sound. Her pain is delicious.

"Daddy! Daddy! *Daddy!*"

Daddy is not a safe word, but it does the trick. I let her go, breathing heavily. Still in control. I resume spanking her. She squirms as the smacks grow harder and closer together, the growl becomes a roar.

Shit. I'm losing it.

I stand up. I'm breathing harder now, like I was in a fight.

The bag. Open the bag.

I pull my gaze away from those sumptuous mounds of flesh and reach down into the bag. My heavy flogger. I lift it out of the bag. Its weight is reassuring. It grounds me. I lightly drag the leather falls from the soles of her feet to the back of her neck and back again. Then I swing it. Hard. It slaps against her ass with a heavy, meaty "Thwack!" Her ass jiggles, and I have to look away for a moment to avoid attacking her right then and there. I strike her shoulders and upper back, careful to avoid her spine. I go back to flogging that beautiful ass. My breath is coming like a steam engine. I toss the heavy flogger aside and reach into the bag for my old flogger, the one I've had since I was twenty, handmade from a tree branch. It is raw and ugly, just like the monster. Just touching it starts the growling again. I can't be certain I ever stopped.

I am less gentle with this one. It strikes her flesh again and again, and she lets out a little moan with each strike. I toss it beside the other and reach in for another. This one has a metal handle with spikes. It is intimidating, medieval, but the falls are thin and soft. Still, I know how to make them sting.

I take a step back so just the tips of the flogger will hit her skin. I swing hard. Air whooshes from her lungs; a growl reverberates from mine. After a few more lashes, I toss it aside too, and pull out my cane.

I tap it up and down her thighs, her ass, back down her thighs. I whack her hard and she curls into a fetal position. I grab her by the ankles and stretch her out again. Then I stripe her legs and ass with the cane until her moans become whimpers. I drop it onto the bed beside the floggers and go for my new paddles.

They are just hours old, purchased yesterday at the fetish flea market, courtesy of my good friend.

She hears the sound of the wood rubbing together and rolls over.

"What have you got there?"

I push her back down onto her belly and hold her down with one hand on her shoulder, forcing her face against the pillow as I give her the first whack of the paddle.

"Oh, Daddy! That stings!"

It is not a complaint. I start with the thin one, going from cheek to cheek. Her ass looks like one big ripe cherry. I grab the larger paddle and bring it down hard on both cheeks at once.

"Daddy!"

She tries to squirm away again, and I pin her down with more force and give her four or five more hard smacks before laying that one aside with the other toys. I laugh. It's a harsh sound, more like a bark. Then I pull out my old paddle, the one that looks like the sole of a boot. I spank her hard with it, watch her claw the sheets, scrambling to get away. My cock is so hard now it's like a weapon. I want to punish her with it, fuck screams out of her. I growl and reach for her. I grab her, sink my teeth into the supple flesh of her hips.

She yelps as I tug at her flesh. The monster inside me wants her flesh. It wants me to tear it from her bones. But I don't. I can't. Back to the bag.

I reach in and retrieve the spiked slapper I bought from another friend. I love this thing. It is one of my new favorites.

I turn it around. No spikes this time. That would end things too quickly. I swing it softly at first, slowly building in intensity until I'm wailing away and she's wriggling and squirming again, trying to get away, and all my instincts are telling me to subdue her. I grab her by the ankles and stretch her out flat once more. She's still struggling, but I hold her in place with my left hand between her shoulder blades, pinning her down as I redden that lovely ass even more. I'm so worked up when I finally let her go that I pull out my cock and begin stroking it as I reach into the bag for the dragon's tail.

The first bite from the dragon's tail immediately starts her shivering. She's in subspace now. I know all her signs. She's riding that wave of endorphins. She wouldn't safe word now if I flayed the skin from her bones. That makes it even more important for me to keep my head.

I lightly touch her with the tip of the tail. Licking her

skin gently with the leather tip, sometimes hard enough to send those shivers down her legs, but not to break skin. It makes such a wonderful sound as it cracks against her lovely alabaster skin, which is now a livid red that makes me think of a ripe crisp apple and makes me wonder again how that sweet flesh would feel between my teeth if this time I bit deeper, felt that splash of blood wash over my taste buds, and tore a chunk out of her. I shake the thought from my head, drop the tail beside the other toys, and grab the dragon's tongue.

It has a metal handle with spikes. A twin to the flogger with the same handle. The tongue itself is made out of black silicone. With just a flick of the wrist I can raise welts or cut skin. I swat her thighs with it and then her ass. I instantly see welts, little angry red stripes that crosshatch her flesh like lines of latitude and longitude. When I finally toss it aside, she is in another universe.

Then I grab the single-tail.

It's a nylon signal whip, handmade, and this is the first time I have used it on a human being. I bought it a month ago, right after the whip class. I have been practicing with it ever since. Yesterday morning I showed my baby how I could crack it so gently that it was like the whisper of a feather. I demonstrated it on a roll of toilet paper, cracking it repeatedly without once ripping the paper. Then I smiled and cracked it one last time, sending confetti into the air. As I crack it this time, and her entire body tenses, I know she is wondering if I will lightly kiss her with it or turn her ass into confetti.

I crack it right where her left ass cheek meets the top of her thigh. Her entire body shakes.

"Oooh, Daddy!"

I growl in response...and crack the whip again. I want her to scream, to cry, to beg me to stop.

Fuck! Eat! kill!

Wait. What did I just think? Dude, that's not cool. Wait,

did my inner voice just call me dude? Why the fuck does my conscience sound like Pauly Shore? I wouldn't kill my baby. I'd fuck her and eat her though.

Dude! That's even worse!

Stop calling me dude! What the fuck am I saying? I'm losing it. Okay, back to the whip. There's a small abrasion in her skin. Not a cut, but just a break in the epidermis, weeping clear plasma. I drop to my knees and lap at it like a thirsty dog. I lick from her calves to the back of her thighs, up the crack of her ass. I rest with my cheek pressed against her ass. It is hot. The heat radiates into me.

"Mmmm. That feels nice," she says.

I lay there for several long moments, until the monster is finally quiet. Then I stand up and pick up all three floggers, one at a time, all three paddles, the cane, the slapper, the dragon's tongue, the dragon's tail, and finally the whip.

"That's the whole damn bag."

She smiles.

"I'm impressed. Now tear me the fuck apart!"

She spreads her legs for me and bends over, ass to the sky. From somewhere deep inside, I feel the monster reawakening. I roar...and attack.

EDIBLE

He wants to objectify her
To reduce her endless chatter
to meat
Organs
Bones
Blood
A sweet succulent thing
he can consume
and not talk
or listen to.

He closes his eyes
Inhales her vanilla skin
And takes another bite
Pain
like August sunshine
So delicious
His taste buds
Burn.

SWITCH

Sheila trembled as Nate tightened the nipple clips, gradually and deliberately turning the little screw on the one attached to her right nipple, while simultaneously turning the one attached to his left. The pain she felt was mirrored in his expression, as was the ecstasy. He closed his eyes and bit his bottom lip as the alligator clamp bit into his pink flesh and hers. Her nipple was turning purple as the circulation was cut off. The dull, stomach-churning pain sent faint tremors through her sex. She was already getting wet...and this was just foreplay.

She tensed as he turned on the violet wand and hooked up an electrode to it, then slowly touched the electrode to the nipple clip attached to her. Twenty thousand volts of electricity arced through her breasts. She gritted her teeth and suppressed a scream. It felt like a thousand needles were jabbing through her aureole. The pain was intense, but not at all unpleasant. The rush of endorphins made her feel like she was high on painkillers, even as pain enveloped her.

It was obvious Nate was enjoying this as well. The chain that linked the two nipple clips carried the electricity to the one attached to him as well. His erection jabbed at the air, looking swollen and angry as jolts of artificial lightning singed his nerve endings and caused his pecs to contract painfully. A droplet of pre-cum glistened on the head of his cock, and Sheila reached out and rubbed it in. His penis glistened with semen as she began to slowly jerk him off, stroking him in long, languid motions. She casually removed the violet wand's attachment from the nipple clip and touched it to Nate's foreskin.

"Oh, fuck! Oh, fuck! Oh, fuck!" he exclaimed, but nowhere in their negotiations had "Oh, fuck" ever been suggested as a safe word. Following her lead, Nate took the electrode from Sheila's hand and touched it to her labia. He turned up the intensity. Thirty-five thousand, forty thousand, fifty thousand volts of electricity seared through her sex. The sensation was like hot scalpels unmaking her vagina in violent slashes. She felt like she was going to bite through her bottom lip, the pain was so overwhelming...so wonderful. Then he slid it up inside her—not the attachment but the whole violet wand. Sheila screamed, grit her teeth, clawed the floor, and came like a river.

Sheila and Nate were both switches, enjoying giving and receiving pain equally, sadomasochists in the most literal sense of the word. Their relationship had always involved competition, from the moment they'd first met in college. Who was the better athlete? Who could get the best GPA? Then who could get the highest paying job? They ran marathons and triathlons, competing to see who could endure the most. Sheila won that competition when she competed in the Bad Water Ultra-Marathon, a 134 mile run through Death Valley in mid-July. Nate had to pull out when he fell to heat exhaustion, but Sheila finished. It wasn't the first time she'd beaten him at something. What good would it have been to compete with an inferior? But this was the first time she had succeeded where he had so utterly failed. Right away she could sense something different about their relationship.

After Death Valley, the competitions had become more... personal. They'd always had an open relationship. They both considered themselves polyamorous. But after Nate's failure in Death Valley, even this had become a contest, a rivalry to see who could acquire the most sexual partners. Sheila had a competitive advantage, of course. Pussy is more highly prized than penis, and men are far less discriminating than women. Nate would have won by a landslide had he been committed enough to victory to suck a cock or two, but being stubbornly heterosexual was a serious handicap, as he discovered one day when he walked in on a gangbang involving Sheila and eight of her closest friends. At least he'd had the good taste to join in rather than interrupt, gracefully conceding defeat by adding his own seed to the glistening mask of semen coating his wife's face and breasts.

When they'd both discovered the wonderful world of kinky sex, he'd thrown himself in wholeheartedly, quickly surpassing her skill at bondage and sadism. She was forced to admit his creativity in the art of inflicting pain greatly rivaled her own. At play parties, he was always a hit among the serious, hardcore masochists who were looking to be flogged and whipped until they were sobbing in agony and bleeding from dozens of welts and lacerations. Rough body play was a specialty of his, and he'd punch and kick subs, hitting every pressure point, not satisfied until he'd forced them to use their safe word. But when it came to receiving pain, Sheila and Nate were equals. They both had extraordinarily high tolerances for even the most excruciating physical trauma. Nate had found this unacceptable. Only total victory would satisfy him after two consecutive crushing defeats.

Nate removed the violet wand from Wanda's vagina as she finished the last of a series of orgasms, and attached one of the leads to a sharp, two-sided dagger. He began cutting Sheila's breasts, bisecting her nipple with the knife's sharp edge as thirty thousand volts of electricity coursed through the blade and into her.

Sheila responded by furiously masturbating as Nate continued cutting. Then it was his turn, and she followed his lead and took the knife and cut on his chest, almost amputating his nipple in a moment of overzealousness. Then she had a better idea. She remembered the little stainless-steel dildo they'd picked up at a famous sex store in San Francisco that was known for vibrators. She unhooked the leads from the knife and attached them to the dildo, and then she told Nate to turn around and began lubing up his anus. He was an anal whore, just like her, and loved to have his prostate stimulated during sex, so this would probably send him into the stratosphere.

Just as she suspected, the moment the electricity hit his prostate, he was shooting an arc of semen halfway across the room. But Sheila wasn't done. She took a small catheter that had come with the violet wand, attached it to the unit, and then turned Nate around. His cock was still pulsing, sticky with semen that still dribbled from the head of his cock. She licked him clean and then sucked him back to full a full erection before easing the electrified catheter into his urethra. That did the trick. He screamed and convulsed, and Sheila was just about to remove it and claim victory when he ejaculated again.

"Oh, God! That was fucking awesome! Your turn."

There was a smaller catheter in the box of violet wand attachments, and Nate removed one and replaced the one sticky with his semen with the clean new one. He leaned Sheila back with her legs splayed wide. She felt him probing around down there, spreading her vulva with his fingers, and then felt white hot agony fire through her sex as the catheter was inserted. Her bowels let loose and urine sprayed all over Nate, who started to laugh uncontrollably.

"Oh, shit! Oh, shit! You fucking pissed on me!"

Sheila started laughing too.

"That's not piss. I'm a squirter."

They both laughed even harder.

"We aren't getting anywhere like this. We're too evenly matched," Nate said as he turned off the violet wand, removed the catheter from Sheila's dripping snatch, and walked into the bathroom to get a towel to clean the urine off his face and hands.

"How about some fire-play?" Sheila asked, calling out to Nate from the bedroom.

"You mean like flash-cotton and fire-cupping? That's more show than go."

"No. I mean like with a blow torch."

Nate paused.

"Are you serious?"

"I'm damn serious."

Nate smiled and walked over to the butane torch they'd purchased at Sears several months ago to burn candles during wax-play. At its very tip, the temperature could reach as high as 3,623°F. Enough to cause third-degree burns in two seconds or burn flesh to a cinder in fewer than three.

"Me first," Sheila said as Nate ignited the flame, and then she began to scream as he lowered it between her legs, and her most delicate flower withered and turned to ash.

SHE WOLF

A cannibal flirtation
a rattlesnake flick of the tongue
Across her meat-stained fangs
in place of a smile

Blood washes down her throat
Like warm red wine
Drools from her chin
In strawberry splatters

Her heart rages
And pushes a quivering scream
Up from her full belly
As the first orgasm
Brings her to her knees

Her body trembles still
As she licks my seed
From her carcass
And smiles
Red and meaty.

THE DEATH OF PASSION

This vicious love of yours
is just another smiling corpse
mutilated and abandoned
by a society that loathes it
and all things feminine
That would see you stripped
of every sensuous curve
reduced
to a bulimic skeleton
Garishly posed
in cabaret colors
and showgirl feathers
covered head to toe
in piss and semen
eyes glued shut
vagina and rectum distended
every orifice plundered
discarded
amongst cigarette butts and beer cans
fast food wrappers and homeless tents
on the side of a busy freeway.
A travesty of wasted wet dreams
and squandered lust.

A parody of romance.
A comedy of sin.
Feeding worms and flowers
with rot and putrescence
Mushrooms growing in your waste
where your legs are splayed akimbo
displaying a formless sexless void
"She"
now a meaningless distinction
others have claimed from you
without deserving
Still trying to seduce and deceive
with no audience but strays and vermin
and leering perverts
They take the best pieces of you
to feed their loathsome offspring
become your vicarious progeny
Rubberneckers gawk as they drive past
Their own lives reaffirmed
by our tragedy.

RAZOR BLADE FUCK TOY

If the immediate and direct purpose of our life is not suffering, then our existence is the most ill-adapted to its purpose in the world: for it is absurd to assume that the endless affliction of which the world is everywhere full, and which arises out of the need and distress pertaining essentially to life, should be purposeless and purely accidental. Each individual misfortune, to be sure, seems an exceptional occurrence, but misfortune in general is the rule.
—Arthur Schopenhauer, Nineteenth-Century Philosopher

The newspapers had been filled with stories of a sadistic serial murderer who tortured his victims for days before they finally died of their injuries. They found the bodies of young men, many of them prostitutes, in dumpsters behind rundown motels in the Tenderloin and Polk Street areas, mutilated beyond all sane imagination. Some were not even recognizable as men.

James was intrigued.

Since he was a teenager, James had been fascinated by serial killers, signature sex killers to be specific. He had no interest in guys like David Berkowitz, who just shot his victims without first torturing them. His interest was in the most sadistic. From Jack the Ripper to Jeffrey Dahmer and the BTK Killer, images of their mutilated victims had filled his fantasies throughout his puberty years and beyond. But his fantasies had never been about hurting people. James wouldn't dream of hurting anyone. He didn't wonder what it felt like to commit such dreadful atrocities against another human being. His preoccupation was with what the victims felt as they were raped, tortured, and dismembered.

***

James was a true sensualist. He delighted in every sensation his body experienced. He accepted and desired pain for its own sake. He lusted for experience at its most extreme. And there is no experience more profound than pain. Pain is the body's warning system that we are doing something, or allowing something to be done to us, that might compromise the integrity of our bodies, that might compromise our lives.

James did not fear death. For him, death was simply the cessation of all sensation, the end of all experience. James had had enough experiences to fill a dozen lifetimes. It was all that could be felt leading right up to that fatal second before the heart stops, that final, dizzying, world-ending anguish that would overload his senses and chase his soul into the ether. That was the experience James craved. The apex of agony, all the human body could sustain before succumbing to madness and death, the limits of human physical endurance. His search had led him to the emergency ward so often that his last trip had ended with a suicide watch and the threat of being locked in a mental hospital. James was a masochist so extreme he'd been banned from every local BDSM group and barred from attending "play parties." What he called "edge-play," most called insanity. Etched into his flesh was an entire history of fathomless joys and agonies,...like hieroglyphics on tomb walls. Dying was the only experience he'd yet to have, the one threshold he hadn't crossed.

He'd been seriously maimed doing a fire-play scene when he'd substituted the 70 percent alcohol usually employed for 100 percent alcohol, leaving third-degree burns on his back and buttocks. Later he'd been banned from a dark party after being flogged with a flogger made of barbed wire and chain. Blood and bits of his flesh had begun to coat the walls, and he'd been forcibly ejected along with his sadistic playmate, who'd burst into tears during the flogging, imploring James to use his safe word. James never did. No one ever saw the man who'd topped him that night again. He'd completely removed himself from the scene and had even deleted his Fetlife profile. There were rumors he'd suffered permanent psychological scars from playing with James. After that, James had taken to playing by himself, all the while fantasizing about the one sadist who would be extreme enough to handle him. It didn't matter to him that the sadist he was looking for just might be the one to end him.

James believed there was no such thing as dying. Until the moment you ceased to exist, you were alive. Once you were dead, there could be no remorse, no regret, because there would no longer be a "you" to feel such emotions. He held the solipsist view that you would not only end, but so would all of time, all of existence, because it only existed as long as you existed to perceive it. Just as Sisyphus accepted his punishment in Hades, endlessly rolling his stone uphill only to watch it roll back down, so did James accept the inevitability of anguish as synonymous with existence. When pain ended, so did life, and James wanted to live! Reality was his playground, an amusement park for his mind, and finding new amusements was his sole preoccupation.

"THE TORTURE KILLER STRIKES AGAIN!
HEADLESS TORSO FOUND IN THE TENDERLOIN!"

James let out a sigh as he took himself in hand and began furiously masturbating as he thumbed through the tabloid, devouring the descriptions of mayhem and carnage as the detectives speculated as to what the victim had endured before being decapitated. James shot a warm stream of semen all over the gory photograph of the corpse as he got to the part where the medical examiner said the victim had been alive during the decapitation. James could scarcely imagine such sublime ecstasy. He'd watched the Taliban and ISIL videos of American captives being crudely and savagely beheaded—with disgust...the first time. He'd wanted to see the bastards who'd done it hunted down and tortured. He'd even hoped for the death of their families. But then...he'd watched them again...and again, unable to help himself. When the videos had finally been removed from the Internet, he'd been relieved. He'd felt wretched taking delight in the misery of those victims, just as he felt wretched about his excitement over the Torture Killer. Every time he had masturbated to those videos, remorse and depression would flood in, crushing him on all sides. He'd felt like a horrible human being, yet he'd continued to do it, waking up each morning, hoping for more news on the Torture Killer, ignoring the fact that more news meant more innocent victims, ignoring the fact that his "pornography" meant the loss of someone's father, brother, husband, lover, or friend. His empathy only returned once his erection had subsided and his semen had been spilled.

After a quick shower, James put on a pair of tight shorts, a tank top, and tennis shoes and then took a taxi to the Tenderloin district. The ride down Market Street was unremarkable. Tourists hurried from one overpriced department store to the next. The homeless sat on sidewalks with hands outstretched, imploring passersby for their spare change. The young urban professionals, software engineers, and tech geeks walked with their heads down, eyes fixed on their smartphones. Hipsters wore skinny jeans and tight T-shirts that barely covered their stomachs. Hip-hoppers wore oversized headphones.

Fat policemen smiled at the female tourists and scowled at and threatened just about everyone else. Gay, lesbian, and heterosexual couples strolled arm in arm, openly displaying their affection for one another with the occasional hug or kiss or tenderly whispered compliment. James absorbed it all silently, staring out the window of the taxi, thoughts still trapped in a spiral of sadomasochism and death.

The taxi dropped him off in front of a dilapidated three-story tenement with a faded sign above the door, which read "York Hotel." He'd been coming down to this same location every night for weeks. Two of the fourteen young male prostitutes known to have been victims of the Torture Killer had worked this very block. James figured it was only a matter of time before the killer returned to claim another victim, and if James was lucky, the killer would choose him this time.

For two weeks, James had found himself wandering the strip. He would stick out his thumb like a hitchhiker, accepting any and every ride offered, hoping to find his destiny, his fatal dream. Thus far he had been robbed five times at the point of a gun, a knife, and a claw hammer. He'd been beaten three times, including by the guy with the hammer, and even raped more than once, but still his prize eluded him.

This time he was standing there for a few brief minutes when a black Cadillac Escalade pulled up beside him. He watched with that familiar excitement, that thrill of anticipation and fear as the window rolled down and a stern face with pale, cadaverous skin and gaunt features peered out at the pedestrians on the sidewalk. The man's eyes slid over the assemblage of preening boy-whores with a carnivorous lust sparkling in his eyes like stars. James thrilled when he saw the man lick his lips, practically salivating, like a starving man at a buffet. The man was a hunter, a hunter of men. James recognized it easily. But was he just hunting for a little boy-pussy, or was he the hunter James had been looking for?

James walked to the curb and stuck out his thumb for a ride. He boldly met the man's intense stare with one he hoped would appear seductive, and then he licked his own painted lips and shamelessly wiggled his ass in the man's direction. The man eyed him suspiciously before swinging the passenger door wide and gesturing for James to join him. James had to fight two other prostitutes who'd attempted to beat him into the Escalade, but James was less street-weary than they and easily fought them off, breathing heavily as he settled in next to the man who looked like the Hollywood stereotype of a mortician: dark suit, pale skin, black hair and eyes, long skeletal fingers. He was straight from Central Casting. This was what serial killers looked like in our imaginations, which immediately made James skeptical. In reality, they didn't look like Snidely Whiplash or Gomez Adams. They were fat, middle-aged men with wives and kids at home, murdering prostitutes in between picking up KFC for dinner, or toothless rednecks getting drunk and torturing female hikers at the deer lease, lonely geeks jacking off to bondage videos in their parents' basement who kidnap and murder their neighbor's kid. They never looked as ominous as this guy. This guy seemed to be trying too hard to look the part. But it was too late now; they were rocketing up Market Street, with the man squeezing James's thigh and occasionally granting him a wan, mirthless smile.

They arrived at his place, a meticulously clean one-bedroom apartment in the Haight-Ashbury district. They kissed, discussed prices, and then adjourned to the bedroom where they began an awkward negotiation. The stern-looking man with the corpse's pallor asked James what his "hard limits" were, and James brazenly replied, "I have none. I'm down for anything."

The man smiled, an expression clearly calculated to appear menacing.

"I'm a sadist. I would like to hurt you."

"I'm a masochist. I'd love you to," James replied with a wink and chuckle.

The man chuckled along with him and then fixed him with those hard eyes once more as all the joy drained from his face. Again it was a deliberate affectation that made James wonder how often the man had practiced that particular expression in the mirror.

"I want to cut you."

James pulled his little shirt over his head, displaying the cuts and welts already festooning his flesh, and then blew the man a kiss. "Please, cut me all you like. I love blood-play."

The man appeared disarmed.

"You have to have *some* limits? Everyone has their limits."

James shrugged. "No one has found them yet. Maybe you'll be the first to find that limit."

"What if I go too far and kill you? What if I want to kill you?"

James shrugged again and let out a sigh. "Then I guess I'll die. Can we get started now?"

"Safe words?"

"Fuck 'em," James replied. "I've never used one."

Excitement leaped into the man's cold eyes, and he strode quickly across the room and pulled a rolling suitcase from the closet, his "toy bag." He opened it with a flourish and began pulling out his toys, laying them out purposefully on a long table by his bed. It was filled with whips and floggers, a cat-o'-nine-tails made of barbed wire, a spiked paddle, knives, scalpels, an ax, and a saw.

James was intoxicated by the sight. He'd found the right man.

"Can I tie you up?"

"Do you really have to ask?"

***

James shivered with delight as the blade traced its way through his flesh. He watched the man with the hard, emotionless eyes, like slivers of glass, lick the blood welling up in his wounds, and goose bumps rose between the welts as he slid a scalpel along James's ribcage. James's arms were bound to his legs, left forearm to left shin and right forearm to right shin, so that he was spread out on the bed with his legs in the air and his genitals exposed. An intricate series of knots began at his wrists and ankles and went all the way up to his elbows and knees. The position was painful, taxing the limits of James's flexibility and cutting off some of the circulation in his arms. But James didn't mind. He'd had worse.

"What should I call you?"

"Death!" The man replied melodramatically as he licked James's blood from the scalpel.

"No, seriously. What's your name?"

"I'm not telling you my name."

"What does it matter? Fine. I'll just call you Sir."

"Call me Death."

"I am *not* calling you Death. I couldn't even say that with a straight face, Sir. You need a good Dom name. You like blood. How about Bloodhound?"

The man paused.

"I like it. You sure it isn't corny?"

James frowned. "Cornier than Death? No, I think it's perfect. Now, hurt me some more, Bloodhound, Sir."

Bloodhound smiled and got back to work. He picked up the leather strop he'd used to sharpen his razor and slapped James across the face with it, splitting James's lip and opening a huge gash in his cheek. He smacked James again and again with the strop, slashing his cheek and spraying blood onto the floor until pink muscle tissue and white bone were visible through the widening avulsion beneath his cheekbone.

James felt the adrenalin, serotonin, and oxcytocin begin to flow from his pituitary gland almost immediately. It wasn't the intoxicating deluge of dopamine and endorphins he craved, however. That would require much more pain, but it was a start. He watched as Bloodhound picked up a cheese grater, a wonderful pervertable if ever there was one, and began sssslowly removing skin from James's chest, cutting through the nipple and nearly shearing it off completely. The sensation was heaven. James floated high on a cloud of morphine-like endorphins as the man he'd christened Bloodhound lifted one of James's fingers, cut around the base of it with his scalpel, and then began peeling the skin off his finger, rolling it up as if removing a condom. The pain was almost too much.

The man looked him in his eyes, studying James's expression as if watching an insect beneath a microscope as he placed James's finger in his mouth and lasciviously sucked the bloodied stump. James shuddered and then giggled as he contemplated the appropriateness of the name he'd given his torturer. He'd hit the nail right on the fucking head. The man was an absolute glutton for blood, just as James was a whore for pain.

James needed this...this agony...the rapturous ecstasy of physical torment. No drug he'd ever found fulfilled him like the ones his body naturally released while being pushed to its breaking point and beyond. He only felt himself truly alive when his senses screamed in anguish. That was when he transcended this drab, banal, flavorless existence for one of light, color, texture, and delirious sensation. What James found hard to conceive of was what sadists got out of it. What did Bloodhound get out of torturing him?

All the experiences were being provided to James. He got the endorphin rush as pain became pleasure in a white hot explosion of overwhelming physical sensation. Bloodhound could feel nothing through his scalpel or the leather strop or even the barbed-wire flogger. As the sadistic serial murderer worked at James's flesh, sending him into some liquid bliss beyond subspace, James stared at the complicated expressions on Bloodhound's face, wondering what he must be thinking. James could see the erection tenting the man's blood-drenched Dockers, but he could not understand it. For James, the blade slicing through his nipple and skinning his chest and stomach like he was peeling an orange was the purest ecstasy, beyond orgasm or the artificial euphoria of opiates or barbiturates. Each cut of the blade through his flesh was like experiencing a lifetime of joys and pains in one razor-sharp moment.

But the blade had no nerve endings to feel its intrusion into James's body. It was not attached to Bloodhound's nervous system in any way. Bloodhound could not feel the sensation of the blade as it opened up James's scrotum so that his testicles plopped out of the sack like oysters shucked from their shells and dangled between his legs on little winding chords of nerves and sinew. He could not feel James's sphincter muscles clench around the blade as it slipped into his anus and cored out his asshole like a half-eaten grapefruit. He could hear James's screams. He could watch James shiver and convulse, his eyes glaze over in a narcotic rapture as the endorphins sent him soaring. Feel the blood wash over his hands or spatter his face as it sprayed from open arteries. But he could only wonder at what James was feeling even as James wondered at the thoughts and emotions driving this sadistic monster.

No sensation the body could produce was more consuming, more overwhelming than the feeling of a sharp blade as it whispered through skin and muscle tissue. Nothing like the anticipation of salacious agony as you watched it cut deeper and deeper, down to the bone. Pleasure was rarely as pleasurable as you expected, and pain was almost always more painful, more intense. Just compare the intensity of emotion experienced by an animal when eating to the animal being eaten. It pales in comparison.

Still, the animal that was making a ruin of James's flesh appeared to be in an ever-increasing state of sexual arousal bordering on orgasmic bliss.

James grit his teeth against the pain as Bloodhound sodomized him with a Bowie knife. James wondered if the man could cum this way. Simply by fucking him with his knife? He wondered if the knife, for this murderous beast, was some type of surrogate penis. Perhaps this was the only way he could fuck? Clearly his penis functioned. James could see the distinct outline of his erection throbbing in his pants. But maybe it only manifested during acts of violence? Maybe the man was not killing him but making love to him the only way he could. James could see no difference between this man with the glazed, half-lidded expression in his eyes, and the way he bit his bottom lip and occasionally closed his eyes completely as he undid James bit by bit, and the expressions he'd seen on the faces of the men he sometimes picked up in bars when they fucked him hard in the ass, sometimes making him bleed, and once sending him to the ER with a prolapsed anus after being fisted by a bodybuilder with hands like George Foreman's.

As the man lit a blowtorch and began heating up the edge of his knife before cutting into James's thighs, cauterizing the arteries even as he sawed through muscle, James was in paradise. He was certain now that he would not survive this encounter. This man was clearly the murderer he sought, and James didn't care. This was what he wanted, to empty his cup of life's elixir, to drink it down to the last drop, and that meant gleefully submitting to all the pain his mortal shell could endure, for that was the very meaning of existence, an unending series of agonies briefly interrupted by periods of joy and ennui. Nearly all pleasure, with exception of sexual pleasure, was merely the lack of discomfort, the absence of pain, a deficit of true experience, a negative rather than a positive. Pain was the only reliably positive sensation, the only true experience. That is why it impresses itself upon living things with greater force and urgency than any other feeling. Just think of how seldom we are aware of our overall good health and physical well-being, but only of that one small physical vexation, that twinge of pain in the lower back, that stiffness in the neck, that spot where the shoes pinch or the underwear chafes. It was these minor discomforts that James had first come to love and learned to delight in.

***

Bloodhound looked down between James's legs and was clearly shocked to see the erection pulsating there despite the blood-loss and the trauma. He sneered in disgust and picked up a flogger made of several lengths of chain and some razor wire. He flogged James's ass and thighs, tearing away large hunks of flesh until he was exhausted from the exertion. Splashes of blood spattered the room, the bed, even Bloodhound.

James lay on the bed trembling and convulsing from the shock, adrenaline, and endorphins had him so high he barely knew where he was anymore.

"That feeeeels sooooo goooood," James crooned, which seemed to make Bloodhound angry. Clearly this was not the reaction he'd been expecting.

After wrapping his hands around James's throat and squeezing until he'd almost crushed his larynx, Bloodhound began to abuse James's erect organ, punching and slapping it before picking up his scalpel and slicing it along the base, slowly peeling the skin off in one long sheath, just as he'd previously done his finger. James moaned in ecstasy as the man rolled the skin up his shaft, using a hemostat to rip it clean off. James couldn't help himself. It was all too much. He ejaculated all over the man's face, eliciting another smack from the razor strop, this time to his naked testicles, which sent a wave of nausea through him and nearly caused him to pass out.

Spots danced before his eyes. His heart raced. His breathing was shallow and rapid, hyperventilating. He took several deep breaths to try to calm himself, struggling to hold onto consciousness, not wanting to miss a moment of torment. His head gradually cleared, leaving only the dull throb in his nuts and the scalding agony in his denuded penis and finger, and the cuts and gouges in his chest and face, all bleeding profusely and saturating the mattress beneath him.

He was still trembling, going into hypovolemic shock when the woman entered the room, a huge woman with fierce, angry eyes and large, pendulous breasts like the Hottentot Venus.

When she smiled, James felt his first true moment of fear in years.

"What the fuck are you two faggots doing?"

She was mammoth, well more than three hundred pounds. Her breasts were the size of Thanksgiving turkeys and hung down to her waistline as if she thought any effort to support them would have been a waste of time. Her legs were like telephone poles crosshatched with spidery, blue varicose veins. Her ass was so wide James could see it while looking at the woman from the front. He smiled. She was beautiful. This was what death should look like. Not like the pale, emotionless ghoul who'd been abusing him for the last half hour, but like this fiery, tribal, primitive goddess of vengeance. Death should be passionate, emotional, as mindless and capricious as life itself.

"I'm going to kill both you cocksuckers!"

And that she was.

The goddess picked up the razor strop and began flailing Bloodhound with it until his hard, cold, dead eyes filled with fear and then tears as he wilted to the floor beneath her onslaught while she alternated between the strop, her fists, and kicking him in the nuts and stomach.

"Is this what you've been up to? Is this why you've been sneaking out every night? So you can play hide the salami with some Polk Street S&M queen?"

The woman was not happy. Her rage was primal and irrational, filled with phlegm-soaked expletives as she bashed Bloodhound in the head with the spiked paddle he'd been meaning to use on James. It was glorious! Strands of peroxide-blonde hair swirled about her head like a fiery halo of white light as she abused her helpless mate. In moments, she had him reduced to a pathetic bleeding child, quivering and sobbing in the corner.

Then she turned toward James. He could tell she wanted to hurt him. He was so excited that all the blood he had not already spilled into the mattress rushed to his penis. He had never seen his dick so hard.

Each step she took toward him sent waves through the gelatinous rolls of fat that wobbled like bags of flesh-colored pudding. Her titanic breasts swayed like wrecking balls. Fat, meaty arms that hung with a curtain of cellulite, like bat wings, reached out to envelop him. Her squinty eyes flashed with goddess-like wrath from deep within the hollow pits formed by her bloated cheeks and low-hanging brow. She removed the scalpel from the floor and licked Bloodhound's blood from it, just as he had licked it clean of James's blood, but the act was not dispassionate when she did it. She salivated over the blade, shivering with some terrifying combination of fury and lust that made James squeal in anticipation.

"Yes! Hurt me. Pleeeeaase, hurt me!"

"Oh, I'm gonna hurt ya, ya little butt-pirate. I'm gonna hurt you reeeeal goood."

***

James watched as the blood-orgy raged on. Bloodhound and his mistress would have both been amazed if they'd known he was still alive and conscious. It should have been impossible, and James knew his vitality was a brief, rapidly eroding phenomenon. He had lost so much blood, and a few vital organs were missing. He had no illusions about his survival chances. He'd been prepared for such an end since he'd read his first true-crime novel about serial killers. This was how he'd always wanted to go.

The goddess was eating what looked like his liver as she rode Bloodhound, whose eyes still looked glassy and dead, but now they were glassy from shock. They were fixed and dilated. He would be dead soon as well. James watched his own lungs expand and contract through the hole in chest where the skin, fat, and muscle had been flensed from his ribcage, pulled back and pinned to the mattress, exposing his beating heart. He watched his heart as it pumped out the last of his life fluid through myriad wounds.

The goddess had James's skinned and severed penis in her hand, using it like some sort of flaccid dildo, attempting to sodomize Bloodhound with it. James imagined he was still attached to it, that he could feel the sensation of the serial killer's puckered anus closing around the head of his cock as it entered him. The goddess was trying in vain to squeeze the bottom of his penis, just above where it had been sliced off, to make a tourniquet out of her meaty fist and hold the blood inside to keep it erect. It wasn't working. The penis went soft and dangled limp from Bloodhound's asshole like a deflated balloon.

The goddess removed the useless organ, yanking it out of Bloodhound's asshole with a wet "pop!" Instead, she lubed up James's fingers with his blood. They were still attached to his amputated arm. Bloodhound seemed to awaken from his fugue state. He whimpered and begged. Tears ran down his face and his bottom lip quivered like a scolded child's. His face reflected a mortal terror so different from the predatory gleam he had previously worn. James imagined this was how his victims must have looked when they knew they were doomed. Unlike James, he had not learned to appreciate life, to understand death, to welcome pain as the culmination of both.

The goddess kissed James's lips, clutched between her plump fingers, and then dropped them to the floor. She continued to ride the horrified serial killer, moaning and crying out like she was in a porno being fucked by John Holmes, while ramming Bloodhound's bleeding anus with James's severed limb. She rubbed James's tongue over her huge, swollen breasts, flicking it across her long, pink nipples with the huge aureoles like slices of bologna, and then down between her thighs. She used the disembodied tongue to lap at her swollen clitoris. The cascade of adipose tissue that hung in successive rows between her chin and the yawning pink maw of her sex, shuddered as she got closer to orgasm.

James was happy he could give this glorious woman such pleasure. He had never been anyone's slave, but if he had, he imagined this would have been the ultimate act of service, giving his mistress one final orgasm with his own dismembered parts as he slipped into oblivion, giving his all for her pleasure.

The goddess screamed as she came and then raised herself up from the man with the haunted eyes, just as he reached his own climax and promptly expired. She plunged

James's tongue up inside her dripping snatch as yet another orgasm rocked her massive form. She smiled at James, her barely alive sex-toy, as she continued to shudder with waves of pleasure.

He had been smiling ever since she'd removed his lips.

ASTRAL PROJECTION

I dream of you
The insanity of the mind at rest
Brings me to you
When the sunlight dies
On moonlit bat wings
At the speed of night
On fast cars
With blaring horns
Screeching tires
And thundering
Radio bass
Rhythm & Blues love songs
That sing of your tears
Twinkling
On your perfect skin
I come to you
Disembodied
As spirit
To take over your flesh
Snuggle up
Close to your soul
And whisper in your heart
"I love you"

I come to you
in chains
Bruised and bleeding
And collapse at your feet
Begging you
to love me back
to love me as deeply
as I love you
I scream myself awake
And find you
Sleeping
Next to me
And you are still
My love
My flesh
My blood
My trembling soul
Is still
Yours.

THE DEATH THROES OF SUMMER

Autumn came with open arteries
Summer gasped
Its dying breath
And all the trees bled out
Gushing like rainwater
The wool fell from his legs
The last sip of wine
Drooled from his blackening lips
And turned the fields brown
With rotting fruit
The cup spilled from his hand
His horns withdrew
Like a shriveling erection
Shocked into retreat
The music screeched
Like injured children
Abused into pre-maturity
The seductive moist lip smile
Fell to a hard line
on the whore's face
as the last
satyr
died.

CRIMES OF PASSION

She expired with a scream
that petite morte
a shudder
and a smile
A sigh
Like the exhausted breath of day
collapsing into night
pain
morphing slowly
into rapture
slipped out between
her clenched teeth
Tears
like crystalline blood
from an ectoplasmic artery
dribbled
down her
cold white cheeks
I kissed away her frigid tears
Kissed her trembling lips
And closed her sorrowful eyes
Forever.

BLEEDING
FOR YOU

I opened every vein I could reach
exsanguinated in strawberry red pools
to feed your endless thirst
became your living
bleeding
Giving Tree
You emptied me.
I murdered all the others
trying to satiate your hunger
yet your stomach still growls
and my blood
is not enough.

HAUNTED

I awake with a start
each morning
to the sound of thunderous footsteps
slamming doors
cries of rage
bitter sighs
flashing lights
fill the room
the cacophony intensifies
I am surrounded
by anger and sorrow
I want to scream
flee
kill
I am trapped
Hounded
Haunted
possessed
Cannot escape
The din of madness
follows me.

THE LAST TIME

Our bodies slammed into one another with an ecstasy and aggression born of the most bizarre marriage of passions. Hatred and Lust. Love and Revulsion. When this salacious violence reached its apex, seven years of love and heartache would bleed out on these sheets, and we would be free of one another. A freedom neither of us wanted but both of us desperately needed, and hated each other for.

We had met at an SLAA meeting—Sex and Love Addicts Anonymous. I stood up to tell the tale of how low I had sunk in my quest to fight off the suicidal loneliness that had followed me since the day I left the womb. Our eyes met as I told that room full of strangers about wandering the streets at two o'clock in the morning searching for some kindred spirit to share my disease with. She understood what I was going through. We had both known pain. It was a perfect marriage.

Our addictions and obsessions had complemented one another. Salena was the most beautiful woman I had ever known. Long, raven-black hair and silvery eyes like a feral cat. Tall, slender body hardened by stress and tension rather than exercise. The sex drive of a teenaged meth addict. Our romance began the moment she stood up to talk about sleeping with one man after another, men who would abuse, humiliate, and mistreat her, just so she could feel like someone loved

117

her. She'd known it wasn't love the men had given her, but it was the closest thing she thought she'd ever find. She'd been wrong. I knew I could love her.

Our strange relationship began with her following me into the men's room and jacking me off in a stall, kneeling before me and letting me ejaculate all over that perfect ecstatic face of hers. We left the twelve-step meeting and walked to my house to find a cure for the loneliness in each other's flesh. Our war began that night as we fell in love with each other's weaknesses, grunting and sweating out our pain, exploiting each other to satiate our pathetic appetites. It would be over when the pain ended.

With nothing more than lust to sustain it, our relationship ceased to grow and rotted on the vine. The conversations stopped. Nothing Salena said or did was a surprise to me. I took it all for granted. I could anticipate every word that came out of her mouth or would ever come out, but I would never know the motivation behind those words. I would never know her true feelings. I would forever doubt her sincerity.

No matter what the poets wrote, no matter how the foolish romantics deluded one another, you can never really know anyone. There is always a barrier between you, keeping you apart. We were separated by skin. She was isolated within hers and I within mine. It maddened and enraged me. I could see the same frustration in her. Every time she tasted my flesh, my semen, every thrust of her hips asked the same question: *Who are you?* She never believed my reply. I couldn't blame her. I didn't believe her either. I didn't want to believe. I wanted to know.

I had to get under her skin, to feel my caresses through the nerves in her flesh, to taste myself through the senses on her tongue, to know how she felt pain, how the moonlight twinkling off the rain puddles in the street looked through her eyes, to know how a smile felt on her face, how her tears felt as they spilled from her eyes, how love felt in her heart, if that love was for me. Love is the desire to unite with the love object, to become one with it in mind, body, and soul. It is an impossible ambition because never can you be certain, 100 percent certain of what another person is thinking or feeling, if the words coming out of their mouths, the expression on their faces bears any similarity to the thoughts in their heads or the emotions in their hearts. The longer you stay with someone, the more apparent this becomes.

Sometimes it happens all at once. You come home to see your loved one packing and realize she's been unhappy with you for the past five years while you've been blissfully unaware. Or you come home to find her dirtying the sheets with some other stud and realize she's been faking orgasms with you for years. Other times it's a gradual thing, a drifting apart, an erosion of emotion as gradual and inevitable as the tide washing away the beach, love finally realizing the futility of its goal and capitulating, becoming something less passionate, less tangible, less real. We had been through all of it and more. Our love was now so deeply married to hatred that the two were indistinguishable. Even now it is difficult to distinguish our love making from mortal combat.

Eventually I gave up trying to know Salena. Her words began to bore me. They meant nothing to me. How could I know what they really meant or if they meant anything at all? It was all just noise to me, like the chirping of a bird, the squeak of a mouse, the bark of a dog, an incomprehensible cacophony. It would drive me mad at times. That's when the arguments would begin. When I couldn't take that dissonant bleating any longer and I would scream at her to "Shut the fuck up!," she would strike me or I would strike her and she would get a knife and I would wind up in the hospital bleeding and explaining to a police officer why I didn't want to press charges. Even through the violence, our sex life had remained passionate. Only when I was enveloped in her flesh did I feel close to Salena.

I stabbed deep into her chalice and stared into her eyes as myriad delirious sensations radiated through my flesh. I felt Salena's skin against my own and it was heaven, but I still was uncertain what my body felt like to her, if she felt anything at all. I punched my turgid flesh deeper between her thighs, feeling satisfied by and then suspicious of her screams. I looked into her eyes and made analogies between her expressions and my own, but it was not a precise science. I knew nothing more than I had when my first thrust burrowed its way inside her, digging a tunnel to her soul, a tunnel never fully completed.

The strength of love is that it is impossible, that it cannot be realized. But we have all fooled ourselves with romance novels and fairy tales into thinking it can. All drives seek their own annihilation. If you are hungry, and you eat, the hunger is gone. If love could achieve its end to make two one, it would dissipate as well. That's what we both wanted. We wanted the love to end. And since lovemaking is the closest approximation two human beings can achieve of a union of two souls, we married our flesh together for this last attempt, to *make* love. To become it. Soon, as our rapture built, all thought of love left us. We drowned in each other's flesh, all identity lost. Washed away on torrents of blood and semen. We had given up on love. What we were doing now was enjoying one last good fuck.

***

We grunted and panted, each thrust drawing more blood, more pain. We had been at it for hours. We were past pleasure as we drowned in it. Love was some distant memory that had lasted only as long as the foreplay. Even our hatred and resentment had not proven resilient enough. It had quickly been immolated in the fires of a deeper, truer animal passion. Growling, biting, scratching, cussing, rutting beasts violently mating as if it would be their last dying act. And it would.

We fucked the sun out of the sky and then back up again without relent. Lust was the only feeling left now as our aggression took the shape of ecstasy, and all of our resentments fell to rapture. All other emotions had been purged from our bodies after the first couple of hours, once the pain had begun. The betrayals, the petty vindictiveness, the abuse had all brought us here, but it would not pull us through. We were lost deep in inherent desires that defied all human understanding, all reason. We had reached our true primal selves. Gone back to nature as beings of instinct and appetite, genetically predisposed to seek pleasure and eschew pain even when the pleasure grew so extreme that it became indistinguishable from agony.

I remember reading about how monkeys wired to a machine that produced an orgasm-like pleasure with the touch of a button had pressed that button until their brains fried, until what had formerly been ecstasy had become screaming torture. Then they pressed it again and again, writhing in nerve-searing anguish until all feeling ended. I remembered this as our bodies slammed together in a vicious collision of quivering flesh. Bathed in blood, semen, and vaginal fluids, as we jack-hammered out each orgasm and sucked and licked out whatever fluids yet remained in our exhausted and agonized bodies. My seed dripped from her lips like a sacrament. Her blood dripped down my thigh like a curse.

By the time our orgasms had begun to run red, our flesh to chafe, rip, and tear, we could no longer remember why we were here or what had brought us. We could no longer remember the arguments that had often ended in verbal and

121

physical abuse. We could no longer remember resolving to put an end to the madness, now that madness had sent us swirling into this maelstrom of skin upon sultry sweating skin, seeking revelation in this wanton lubriciousness that had so quickly degenerated into carnage. Now that we swapped pleasure, pain, and body fluids in what no longer resembled sex so much as warfare. Now that we tore at each other, I with a blade I'd hidden between the mattress and box spring and she with some slender dagger she'd hidden beneath her pillow, we could only wonder if perhaps we had touched on some higher plane, shared the same thought. I wanted to get inside her, to touch her heart, even if I had to cut my way to it. It seems Salena had the same plan.

We filled the bed with a tidal wave of arterial blood in a carnivorous rapture that would never again resemble lust so much as primal hunger. I bit off her nipples and began to devour her tender breasts. Each bite of her succulent flesh was heaven. Ecstasy. She tore open my scrotum with her sharp nails and ripped off my testicles in what would never again bring pleasure but only fathoms of pain. Our bodies opened red like roses in bloom, and we tried to crawl within one another. I wanted to crack open her ribcage and nestle in her chest cavity, to lay my head against her heart and listen to it pump out the last of her blood.

I felt her blade cut into me and met her thrust with my own. She fucked me hard and fast with her slender dagger, and I opened wider to accept more of her remorseless passion. Then we began to feed.

We cannibalized each other. I devoured her breasts and buttocks, chewed off each silken fold of her labia, and she swallowed my rigid, blood-gorged flesh and bit it off at the root. I imagined I could still feel my penis as it slid down her throat and into her stomach. Each bite brought us closer to that union of body and soul we'd always desired. Bit by bit she masticated and swallowed me. I nestled contentedly in her stomach where she slowly assimilated my flesh with hers. I did the same to her, finally opening her up and seeing her true essence in wet red, gobbling up her tender organs as she moaned and screamed, delirious in pain and rapture. Our identities dissolved; reality began and ended where we joined. The whole world receded, no longer a consideration at all now that we were of one flesh.

I stabbed deeper into her and found that this tunnel had no light at its end, found that this darkness had no end, that this last little death would be final. In what no longer felt like lust so much as love.

"I love you," she gurgled through a lungful of blood.

I love you too, I thought in return even as I slipped away.

SOMETIMES

Love is so profound
You have to hurt
to feel it
A bite
A spank
my hand around your throat
Is how you know
you're special
A crack
A lash
a stroke from my cane
Is more intimate than a kiss
A bruise
a welt
a slowly healing cut
Is all the adornment
your lovely flesh requires
Your moans
Your screams
A safe word never spoken
And I forget there was life
before you.

WRATH JAMES WHITE is the author of *The Resurrectionist, Succulent Prey, Yacob's Curse, Sacrifice, Pure Hate,* and *Prey Drive (Succulent Prey Part II)*. He is also the author of *Voracious, To The Death, Skinzz, The Reaper, Like Porno for Psychos, Everyone Dies Famous In A Small Town, The Book of a Thousand Sins, His Pain,* and *Population Zero*. He is the co-author of *Teratologist* co-written with the king of extreme horror, Edward Lee, *Orgy of Souls* co-written with Maurice Broaddus, *The Killings* and *Hero* co-written with J.F. Gonzalez, *Son of a Bitch* co-written with Andre Duza and *Poisoning Eros I and II* co-written with Monica J. O'Rourke.

His short stories have appeared in several dozen magazines and anthologies. In 2010, his poetry collection, *Vicious Romantic* was nominated for a Bram Stoker Award.

deadite press

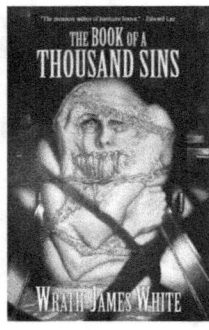

"The Book of a Thousand Sins" Wrath James White - Welcome to a world of Zombie nymphomaniacs, psychopathic deities, voodoo surgery, and murderous priests. Where mutilation sex clubs are in vogue and torture machines are sex toys. No one makes it out alive – not even God himself.

"If Wrath James White doesn't make you cringe, you must be riding in the wrong end of a hearse."
        -Jack Ketchum

"Population Zero" Wrath James White - An intense sadistic tale of how one man will save the world through sterilization. *Population Zero* is the story of an environmental activist named Todd Hammerstein who is on a mission to save the planet. In just 50 years the population of the planet is expected to double. But not if Todd can help it. From Wrath James White, the celebrated master of sex and splatter, comes a tale of environmentalism, drugs, and genital mutilation.

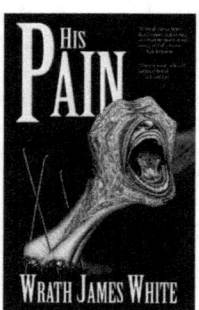

"His Pain" Wrath James White - Life is pain . . . . . . or at least it is for Jason. Born with a rare central nervous disorder, every sensation is pain. Every sound, scent, texture, flavor, even every breath, brings nothing but mind-numbing pain. Until the arrival of Yogi Arjunda of the Temple of Physical Enlightenment. He claims to be able to help Jason, to be able to give him a life of more than agony. But the treatment leaves Jason changed and he wants to share what he learned. He wants to share his pain . . . A novella of pain, pleasure, and transcendental splatter.

"Like Porno for Psychos" Wrath James White - From a world-ending orgy to home liposuction. From the hidden desires of politicians to a woman with a fetish for lions. This is a place where necrophilia, self-mutilation, and murder are all roads to love. Like Porno for Psychos collects the most extreme erotic horror from the celebrated hardcore horror master. Wrath James White is your guide through sex, death, and the darkest desires of the heart.

"Son of a Bitch" Andre Duza and Wrath James White - Demitrius is a son of a bitch. He breeds vicious dogs for drug-dealers and dog-fighters. But one dog came out very wrong. It is less an animal and more a beast from the depths of hell. This creature perfectly suits Warlock, a local hitman, for a unique purpose. The hitman's conscience ends up trapped in the demon dog's body and the two begin to merge into one will hunt the town and exact vengeance upon all those that cursed it to this fate worse than death.

"The Innswich Horror" Edward Lee - In July, 1939, antiquarian and H.P. Lovecraft aficionado, Foster Morley, takes a scenic bus tour through northern Massachusetts and finds Innswich Point. There far too many similarities between this fishing village and the fictional town of Lovecraft's masterpiece, The Shadow Over Innsmouth. Join splatter king Edward Lee for a private tour of Innswich Point - a town founded on perversion, torture, and abominations from the sea.

"Mangled Meat" Edward Lee - No writer is more hardcore, offensive, or notorious than Edward Lee. His world is one of torture, bizarre fetishes, and alien autopsies. Prepare yourself, as these three novellas from the king of splatterspunk are guaranteed to make you gasp, gag, and laugh your ass off. Featuring "The Decortication Technician," "The Cyesolagniac," and "Room 415."

"Necro Sex Machine" Andre Duza - America post apocalypse...a toxic wasteland populated by bloodthristy scavengers, mutated animals, and roving bands of organized militias wing for control of civilized society's leftovers. Housed in small settlements that pepper the wasteland, the survivors of the third world war struggle to rebuild amidst the scourge of sickness and disease and the constant threat of attack from the horrors that roam beyond their borders. But something much worse has risen from the toxic fog.

THE VERY BEST IN CULT HORROR

deadite press

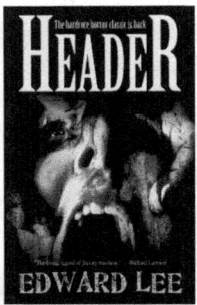

"Header" Edward Lee - In the dark backwoods, where law enforcement doesn't dare tread, there exists a special type of revenge. Something so awful that it is only whispered about. Something so terrible that few believe it is real. Stewart Cummings is a government agent whose life is going to Hell. His wife is ill and to pay for her medication he turns to bootlegging. But things will get much worse when bodies begin showing up in his sleepy small town. Victims of an act known only as "a Header."

"Red Sky" Nate Southard - When a bank job goes horrifically wrong, career criminal Danny Black leads his crew from El Paso into the deserts of New Mexico in a desperate bid for escape. Danny soon finds himself with no choice but to hole up in an abandoned factory, the former home of Red Sky Manufacturing. Danny and his crew aren't the only living things in Red Sky, though. Something waits in the abandoned factory's shadows, something horrible and violent. Something hungry. And when the sun drops, it will feast.

"Zombies and Shit" Carlton Mellick III - Twenty people wake to find themselves in a boarded-up building in the middle of the zombie wasteland. They soon discover they have been chosen as contestants on a popular reality show called Zombie Survival. Each contestant is given a backpack of supplies and a unique weapon. Their goal: be the first to make it through the zombie-plagued city to the pick-up zone alive. But because there's only one seat available on the helicopter, the contestants not only have to fight against the hordes of the living dead, they must also fight each other.

"All You Can Eat" Shane McKenzie - Deep in Texas there is a Chinese restaurant that harbors a secret. Its food is delicious and the secret ingredient ensures that once you have one bite you'll never be able to stop. But when the food runs out and the customers turn to cannibalism, the kitchen staff must take up arms against these obese people-eaters or else be next on the menu!

"Whargoul" Dave Brockie - It is a beast born in bullets and shrapnel, feeding off of pain, misery, and hard drugs. Cursed to wander the Earth without the hope of death, it is reborn again and again to spread the gospel of hate, abuse, and genocide. But what if it's not the only monster out there? What if there's something worse? From Dave Brockie, the twisted genius behind GWAR, comes a novel about the darkest days of the twentieth century.

"Bigfoot Crank Stomp" Erik Williams - Bigfoot is real and he's addicted to meth! It should have been so easy. Get in, kill everyone, and take all the money and drugs. That was Russell and Mickey's plan. But the drug den they were raiding in the middle of the woods holds a dark secret chained up in the basement. A beast filled with rage and methamphetamine and tonight it will break loose. Nothing can stop Bigfoot's drug-fueled rampage and before the sun rises there is going to be a lot of dead cops and junkies.

"The Dark Ones" Bryan Smith - They are The Dark Ones. The name began as a self-deprecating joke, but it stuck and now it's a source of pride. They're the one who don't fit in. The misfits who drink and smoke too much and stay out all hours of the night. Everyone knows they're trouble. On the outskirts of Ransom, TN is an abandoned, boarded-up house. Something evil happened there long ago. The evil has been contained there ever since, locked down tight in the basement—until the night The Dark Ones set it free . . .

"Genital Grinder" Ryan Harding - *"Think you're hardcore? Think again. If you've handled everything Edward Lee, Wrath James White, and Bryan Smith have thrown at you, then put on your rubber parka, spread some plastic across the floor, and get ready for Ryan Harding, the unsung master of hardcore horror. Abandon all hope, ye who enter here. Harding's work is like an acid bath, and pain has never been so sweet."*
- Brian Keene

AVAILABLE FROM AMAZON.COM